*Look what people are saying
about these talented authors!*

**Betina Krahn**

"One of the genre's most creative writers.
Her ingenious romances always entertain
and leave readers with a warm glow."
—*RT Book Reviews*

"Nothing could be better about this book.
It's a keeper."
—*RT Book Reviews* on *Make Me Yours*

**Joanne Rock**

"Joanne Rock has a home run of a hit
with four sexy, hotter than hot players."
—*The Belles & Beaux of Romance* on
*Sliding into Home*

"Four fabulous tales! The sex is scorching and
the four couples are engaging and entertaining."
—*Romance Reviews Today* on *Sliding into Home*

**Lori Borrill**

"Bright, humorous and with great dialogue and
situations, this book is a keeper."
—*RT Book Reviews* on *The Personal Touch*

"Romance, great characters and humor all combine
in *Unleashed* by Lori Borrill. This wonderful story
is one you will probably want to reread."
—*RT Book Reviews*

## ABOUT THE AUTHORS

Bestselling author **Betina Krahn** is the mother of two and the owner of two (humans and canines, respectively) and the creator of dozens of satisfying happily ever afters. Her historical romances have received numerous reviewer's choice and lifetime achievement awards and have appeared regularly on bestseller lists...including the *USA TODAY* and *New York Times* lists. Her books have been called "sexy," "warm," "witty" and even "wise." But the description that pleases her most is "funny"— because she believes the only thing the world needs as much as it needs love is laughter. Visit her online at www.BetinaKrahn.com to learn more about her and her books.

Three-time RITA® Award nominee and Golden Heart winner **Joanne Rock** is the author of more than forty books for Harlequin. A romance fan since forever, Joanne liked to tuck romance novels in her school backpack to read after completing the day's lessons, and she is certain that her extra reading improved her school skills tremendously. (Just ask her three sons who've heard her preach this since birth.) When she's not writing or chatting with fans, Joanne teaches English at the local university to share her love of the written word in all its forms. For more information visit Joanne at www.JoanneRock.com.

An Oregon native, **Lori Borrill** moved to the Bay Area just out of high school and has been a transplanted Californian ever since. She credits her writing career to the unending help and support she receives from her husband and real-life hero. When not sitting in front of a computer, she can usually be found at the baseball fields playing proud parent to their son. She'd love to hear from readers and can be reached through her Web site at www.LoriBorrill.com.

# Betina Krahn
# Joanne Rock, Lori Borrill
## MANHUNTING

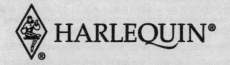

### HARLEQUIN®

TORONTO • NEW YORK • LONDON
AMSTERDAM • PARIS • SYDNEY • HAMBURG
STOCKHOLM • ATHENS • TOKYO • MILAN • MADRID
PRAGUE • WARSAW • BUDAPEST • AUCKLAND

Recycling programs for this product may not exist in your area.

ISBN-13: 978-0-373-79523-9

MANHUNTING
Copyright © 2010 by Harlequin Books S.A.

The publisher acknowledges the copyright holders of the individual works as follows:

THE CHASE
Copyright © 2010 by Betina Krahn.

THE TAKEDOWN
Copyright © 2010 by Joanne Rock.

THE SATISFACTION
Copyright © 2010 by Lori Borrill.

# CONTENTS

For Joanne Rock and Lori Borrill,
terrific writers and fun collaborators.

And, of course, for Brenda Chin,
whose discerning eye makes all of
our stories better.

# THE CHASE
Betina Krahn

# *Prologue*

"THREE HOT BABES ON Valentine's Day!" Barry the bartender spread his arms and grinned. "Heaven got my order straight."

Samantha Drexel stopped in the middle of sliding onto a stool at the end of the convention hotel bar. Him again. Her gaze fell to the prominent slice of uber-hairy chest where his oversize Italian horn amulet rested. Mr. I'm-Too-Sexy-For-My-Shirt.

"I'm afraid we're not here to answer your prayers," she said, turning to her two friends with a *stay or go?* look.

"He's harmless," Tori Halsey said, tossing back her long blond hair.

"Ouch." Barry clapped a hand over his heart.

"He's good for a laugh." Kitty Clayborn's dark eyes twinkled.

"Double ouch." He crossed that hand with the other.

"Tonight he's also good for a drink," said Manny, a fellow bartender, reaching over Barry's shoulder to stuff a twenty into his shirt pocket. "He just won twenty bucks on you three."

Barry's lounge lizard smile froze.

"You *bet* on us?" Samantha looked from Barry to her friends with exaggerated outrage. "He *bet* on us."

"Well, I figured you'd be back. You're always here on Valentine's Day. What—like three years running?" Barry finally realized he was digging himself deeper. "I mean, you never have dates or anything."

A hand grenade dropped in their midst couldn't have had any more effect than that simple declaration.

"Hello. *At a trade show here. Working.*" Sam charged into the deepening silence. "Plus, we're in the 'greetings' industry. Corporate—" she pointed to herself and then each of the others in turn "—freelance and retail. Valentine's Day is our *business.*"

The three had met four years ago at the Greeting Card Association's Winter Trade Show in Dallas, perversely always held over the industry's big Valentine's holiday. Bonding over drinks and dinner on that first night, they had quickly gone from business contacts to fast friends.

"Yeah, we always have to work," Kitty declared.

"Besides, we have standards," Tori put in, with a glance at the dregs of the happy-hour crowd propped up along the hotel lobby bar.

"So I think you *do* owe us a drink," Sam said with a defiant edge.

"And you can bring them to that table—" Tori pointed "—over there."

By the time they had ordered and settled around the nearby table, Sam's mind was in overdrive, unable to let go of Barry's words.

"'Never have dates,'" she quoted, scowling. "Do you believe that guy?" But how long had it been since she was out on an honest-to-goodness date? Dinner, a show or concert, and sweating up some sheets afterward?

"I have dates. Plenty of dates," Tori said, frowning. "Until lately. I guess I've been kind of caught up in my work."

"In a small town—" Kitty sighed "—there's not much to choose from. It's been a major dry spell for me. I could use a good 'bump in the junk.'"

Sam and Tori hooted laughs.

"I think what you mean is 'a bump in your trunk,'" Tori said.

"Are you sure?" Kitty scowled. "Some girls were in the store the other day talking lyrics, and I'm pretty sure they said 'bump in the junk.'"

"Trust Tori on this," Sam said. "She knows her *trunk* from her *junk*."

"Great," Kitty muttered. "If I did actually 'get me some' I probably wouldn't know where to put it."

There was shared pain in their laughter. In the three years they'd been meeting at the Dallas trade show, none of them had been in a real relationship. If Sam weren't so rational, she'd wonder if working in the Valentine's Day trade had somehow jinxed their love lives.

"So if we did hook up with a Valentine's date, how would we celebrate?" Sam cut a sideways look at the red foil hearts taped up here and there around the bar. "Living with mushy poems and romance-y visuals year-round pretty much spoils the prospect of the usual card and heart-shaped box of candy."

"Not with *roses*, that's for sure." Kitty brought up another Valentine's Day staple. "Those big, woody red things they hijack people into paying a hundred dollars a dozen for—they're mutants. The smell's been bred completely out of them."

Sam's thoughts went inescapably to the only bouquet of roses she had ever gotten on Valentine's Day…her junior year of college…just before her boyfriend Rich Collier's big fraternity dance…

"Here you go!" At that moment Barry arrived at their table with a tray of drinks. When they looked up, there was a sagging red rose between his teeth. Plopping the limp flower—clearly plucked from a nearby hotel arrangement—on the table, he leaned in with a suggestive waggle of the eyebrows. "For my favorite sexy babes."

They glanced at each other and laughed guiltily.

Thinking they were awed by his smooth line, Barry laid out their drinks and then swaggered off as if he assumed that—behind his back—they were admiring his butt every step of the way.

"Well, he got one thing right," Sam said, hoisting her gin and tonic with a wicked laugh. "We *are* sexy babes."

Kitty nearly snorted her white wine out her nose.

"I'm serious. Look at you," Sam said, gesturing to her friends. "Tori's got that whole 'bohemian chic' thing going…the flowing blond hair and silk scarf shirts and exotic jewelry…not to mention the killer body. And Kitty's a Ralph Lauren dream…all horse-country casual in boots and blazers…with the pouty lips Hollywood pays big money for."

"And you, Miss Corporate Cool—" Tori picked it up "—with the auburn hair and Lauren Bacall voice…and legs up to the forty-fifth floor. You're not so bad yourself."

"My point exactly. We deserve some Valentine's Day rapture," Sam said, snapping the red plastic heart off the top of her swizzle stick.

"So," she continued, "what was your best Valentine's Day ever?"

After a moment, Tori laughed and launched into a story about sneaking downstairs to her older brother's Valentine party and seeing his best friend making out with a girl on the stairs.

As she listened, Sam's thoughts went inescapably back to the day she'd received that first and only bouquet of roses. The Valentine's Dance had been magical. She'd never forgotten the sight of Rich standing at the bottom of the staircase holding a single red rose to match the ones he had sent her, looking for all the world like Brad Pitt in *Legends of the Fall.*

By the time Kitty related her story about making a Valentine dinner that ended with a sinful chocolate cake, sinfully consumed…Sam was also remembering the fight she and Rich had after the dance. It was supposed to be their first time, but Rich hadn't brought condoms and she hadn't yet started the pills she'd gotten from the Student Health Center…

Strange how she still thought of him whenever she saw a bouquet of roses in a magazine, on television or on a co-worker's desk. Her first love. Nothing since had quite measured up to it for sheer thrill power.

A moment later that thought horrified her.

"Your turn," Tori was saying as she came back to the present.

"My best Valentine's Day—is yet to come," she said forcefully. "Not that I don't love you guys, but next year I'll have a *date*. I'm going to go out and track one down and have a fabulous hot Valentine's night."

"Track one down? Like, you're going *hunting* or something? For a *man?*" Tori said, trying to wrap her head around the concept.

*"Manhunting?"* Kitty looked mildly alarmed. "Just how do you intend to go about that? I mean, lurking around gyms and football stadiums with a club in hand can get you arrested."

When they stopped laughing, Sam's mind hit high gear.

"It's just like business…there are opportunities all around. You have to keep your eyes and mind open to find them. There are single men in fitness centers, bookstores, home improvement classes, volunteer jobs. Put the word out with friends at work, neighbors, old classmates. Sign up for an Internet 'match' service or one of those just-lunch things. Take charge. Decide what you want and go for it."

*"Manhunting."* Tori caught her enthusiasm. "I like it. Sounds primal. Very woman power. I'm in."

Grinning, Sam put out her hand. Tori took a deep breath and put hers on top. They both turned to Kitty, who groaned but added her hand to the pile. "Three, two, one," Sam counted down.

"Manhunting!" they shouted in unison…just as Barry arrived with a tray of fresh drinks.

Moments later he was back behind the bar, disappointed by their lack of response to his irresistible lines. His fellow bartender, Manny, met him at the central beer taps and nodded to the Valentine threesome.

"What was all that about?"

"Them?" Barry gave a huff and began clearing empties from the bar top. "They just made some girl pact. They're going *manhunting.*"

"Your Valentine hotties?" Manny chuckled. "Where do I sign up?"

"They say they're not spending another Valentine's Day here, alone. They're gonna go out and find true love." He gave a snort of disbelief. "*Fifty* bucks says they'll be back next year."

# 1

"WHAT DO YOU MEAN, he didn't show up?" Sam Drexel stopped dead in the middle of the polished executive hallway of the CrownCraft offices, causing two people behind her to have to scramble to avoid a collision.

The renowned L.A. photographer on the other end of the call declared he had waited for three full hours before shutting down his equipment and letting his crew go. And, no, he was *not* available for a reschedule. But, yes, he would be sending her the *full* bill. The last thing Sam heard as he hung up was "damned rock stars."

*Damned rock stars.* The words drummed in her head as she punched her phone off, did an about-face and made straight for the elevator. Part of her was reeling, but part of her was already calculating how much damage this would do to her strained project budget. What kind of jerk blew off a photo shoot costing tens of thousands of dollars? Who the hell did he think he was?

But the minute she stepped out of the elevator on the thirty-eighth floor—home of CrownCraft's marketing department—the sounds of Nick Stack's music throbbing through the corridors reminded her exactly who the hell he was. The king of the driving-hot beat and libido-ramping lyrics. The master of sexy signature sounds. The pied piper of rock, who led impressionable young college girls into a labyrinth of desire and sexual discovery. At least, *he used to.*

She told herself that her heart was racing because she was angry—justifiably so. But her footsteps synchronized with the music, and by the time she reached the marketing department workroom she had to stop and lean against the wall to collect herself. The bass-heavy rush of Nicholas Stack's biggest hit invaded her skin, loosened her bones and threatened to take over her heartbeat.

Damned music. She was determined not to let her potent visceral reaction to it undercut her anger.

*He hadn't even shown up.*

Taking a deep breath, she rolled around the door frame and charged into the workroom, coming to a stop with her hands on her hips.

"Will somebody turn off that howling before I throw the damned speakers out the window?"

Her assistant and the two designers on the floor in the midst of a sea of greeting card layouts looked up in surprise. Parts of the sexy groove thumping away on the stereo would soon fill a number of the musical valentines spread in a mock-up stage all around them. And the whole project, especially the music, had been *her* idea.

As they shook their heads in disbelief, her face reddened. She couldn't blame them for being confused. Two months ago she couldn't get enough of Nick Stack's steamy ballads and sexed-up dance numbers, and had even broken into a few exotic dance moves during his vocal riffs.

She lunged for the off button in the middle of one of Stack's patented, knee-weakening *"bay-beeee's,"* and the silence that followed was so deep it seemed as if the room had just been dropped down a well.

"Whoa." Dale Emerson pushed away from the worktable. The project's head designer wore a gray-streaked ponytail and was talented enough to get by with saying whatever he thought. "What set you off?"

"He didn't show," she said, her face now glowing hot. "Stack didn't bother to put in an appearance at the photo shoot this afternoon. So, as of now, we have no poster, no ads and no CD cover."

"But we've *got* to have photos," graphic artist Sarah Casey moaned.

"The jerk didn't even call to make excuses," Sam said, surveying the line of cards at her feet and feeling the pride she'd taken in the concept being eroded by an all-too-personal feeling of betrayal.

"Why would he miss a chance for such publicity?" her assistant, Renee Morgan, asked.

"Besides the obvious? That he thinks the whole world revolves around him? Who knows?" Sam squeezed her eyes shut for a moment, then expelled a huge breath. "I *hate* Valentine's Day."

"We've noticed." Dale tried to lighten the mood. "And why is that? Not enough valentines in your shoe box in the third grade?"

"I got *plenty* of valentines, Dr. Freud." She crossed her arms and focused an incendiary gaze on one particularly romantic-looking layout. "I just get sick of seeing sappy red hearts wherever I look and hearing songs that rhyme 'baby' with 'lay me.'"

She realized they were giving each other speaking looks and struggled to give her reaction a more businesslike slant. "Besides, the Valentine's campaign is a pink collar ghetto. Have you noticed that they always give it to a woman? Me, specifically? Three years running?"

"Maybe they give it to you because you do such a good job with it." Sarah held up a pair of layout boards in evidence. "I mean, these are damned good designs and the music you chose fits so perfectly—"

"Face it, kiddo," Dale said with a hint of mischief. "There

just aren't many Wharton MBAs around with a great eye for 'romantic.'"

Sam flinched. Stiffening, she turned on her heel and strode out, but not before she heard a chuckle and Dale's irreverent conclusion.

"*Somebody* needs a date."

So much for keeping it strictly professional.

This whole project had become a cautionary tale on the hazards of mixing her professional life with her personal one. If she hadn't been floating around in a romantic fog, she would never have gotten the bright idea to build a line of musical valentines around Nick Stack's signature sounds and phrases.

By the time she got to her office and slammed the door, she was trembling. Renee, Dale, Sarah…everybody knew her love life had gone to hell. How could they not? She was riding a romantic skyrocket one week and barely dragging her butt into work the next. She caught her reflection in the window as she headed for her chair.

She was on edge. Overworked. Exhausted.

*Embarrassed.*

The memory she'd been trying to suppress boiled up to threaten her composure. Rich Collier—bouquet-of-roses Rich—had been in Chicago on business and given her a call out of the blue.

She winced. Okay, not exactly "out of the blue." She had let an old classmate know she was interested in finding out what had happened to her ex-boyfriend, and a month later— *voilà*—he called. Apparently he thought they had unfinished business, too. She'd taken it as proof that her manhunting strategy of "mining the list of old boyfriends" was a winner.

*Manhunting.*

What the hell had she been thinking?

As if decent, rational, gainfully employed heterosexual

males just roamed the landscape, waiting to be bagged, banded and domesticated.

She refused to allow the pricking in her eyes to turn into tears. Two doors down, somebody punched the play button again and Nick Stack's smoky, compelling invitation filtered through her office walls…muted, but still powerful enough to conjure the memory of Rich showing up at her apartment that first night with "their album." A few bars of that sexy, driving beat and that mesmerizing voice, and she was putty in his hands.

It was the music.

It got into her blood and lowered her defenses. It always had. She couldn't help thinking that she hadn't fallen in love with Rich Collier so much as she had been seduced by that damned music—*twice*.

Still, she should have known something wasn't right. Who the hell left Chicago on the weekend to go home to Muncie, Indiana? Nobody. Unless he was expected home on Friday evening. By his *wife*.

Where was her judgment, her business-honed instinct for subtext, nuance and deception? Where was her bullshit meter when she needed it?

*Drowned out by raging hormones, a scorching set of male vocals and a hypnotic 4/4 beat.*

What was the female equivalent of "thinking with your dick"?

Crimson with humiliation, she hit the intercom and dug deep into her reserves for some heavy-duty attitude.

"Get me somebody in Legal," she ordered when Renee answered. "Nick Stack is going to rue the day he violated this contract."

*Four weeks later*

"This goes against everything I'm trying to do, Stan." Nick Stack stopped in the middle of the sidewalk as they emerged from the Drake Hotel on Chicago's Miracle Mile. His leather jacket collar was flipped up against the November wind, his shaggy hair was blowing wildly, and his glare was hot enough to sear meat…all of which made him look very bad-boy rocker. A label he no longer appreciated.

"It's *money,* Nick." Agent Stanley Ripken waved his client toward the limo waiting at the curb with the door open. When Nick balked, Stan produced a glare from under wiry brows. "Get in the damned car."

"They'll flash these pictures all over the country," Nick growled.

"We should be so lucky. It's called publicity. And you need it."

"Not like this, I don't. It's my old sound. I'll never be taken seriously in jazz until that crap is six feet under."

"After this shoot, they'll cut you a nice check and we'll hold a nice wake. Then you'll get on with the new demo, and we'll all get rich again."

"Is that all you think about? Money?"

Stan squared on him, glaring.

"No. Right now I'm thinking of a photo shoot that you blew off and a lawyer screaming in my ear about failure to perform contracted services. You told me to get you some money—I got you some. 'Just tell me where to show up,' you said. *Only you didn't show up!*" Then, like the father figure he'd often been to Nick, he pointed to the open car door. "Quit being such a diva and get in the car."

Muttering, Nick climbed into the back of the limo. This, he told himself, was payback for all the pointless excesses of his former career. He was having his crimes against music and artistic integrity emblazoned on a valentine and hung around his neck for the whole world to see.

Stan was right—this was his fault. He needed money for

a new demo album and was desperate enough to think he didn't care how he got it.

It turned out he did care. A lot.

But his boycott of the L.A. photo shoot had only made matters worse. When they demanded a reshoot, CrownCraft insisted it be done in Chicago so it could be properly "handled" by their marketing department.

When the car stopped in front of a skyscraper, Nick rolled out and stood looking up at the place in horror. Sixty glass-paneled floors of tedium. He groaned. His last photos as an A-lister had been shot by an up-and-comer in Greenwich Village who took him out on the street—shirtless and holding his guitar—and captured what happened as he stopped traffic and sent most of lower Manhattan into gridlock. Now he was so far off the cutting edge that he was being funneled into an advertising photographer's queue…just after the laundry soap and right before the mouthwash.

In that delightful state of mind, he emerged from the elevator onto the thirty-second floor and found a woman in a steel gray suit waiting with feet spread, arms crossed and chin out. Her auburn hair was pulled back into a ponytail. She had damned fine legs—what he could see of them—and an attitude like the helmeted fat lady out of a Wagnerian opera. She was a little intimidating…and sexy as hell.

"We've been waiting," she said in a deep, resonant voice that made his ears tingle.

"You know what they say. 'Good things come to those who wait,'" Stan said with his most disarming smile.

"Whereas, we get *your client*." She shot Nick a glare that sent a jolt of electricity through him, then turned briskly toward a nearby hallway.

This was his "handler"? Nick shook off the lingering sensual buzz, stuck his hands in his pockets and stalked after Stan and the Dungeon Mistress. Clearly, she wasn't a fan.

Probably a major corporate ladder climber. She sure had the legs for it. He followed them down to a pair of black spike heels with wicked red soles. There were probably men all over CrownCraft with matching puncture marks on their backs.

Watching the sway of her prime asset down the long hallway, he found himself experiencing a growing tension…in response to her hostility or her long-legged presence? Given the fact that this was photo shoot number *two*, it was undoubtedly the former. Her dismissive look and snide comment said clearly that she doubted they were going to get their money's worth. And that came as something of a shock to him. Women usually appreciated him. In fact, they generally threw themselves at—

He slid his hand to his chest to explore the odd sensation developing there, then caught himself, scowled and jammed it back into his pocket.

Who the hell was she to…

He glared at her erect shoulders and superbly toned butt.

Fine. She expected a rock star—by damn, he'd give her a rock star. A no-holds-barred bad boy with ego and libido run amuck. With a little luck, the experience would be so obnoxious and the photos so bad that the company would use them sparingly…or not at all. Just what he wanted.

Brunhilda led them into a warehouse-size studio that was already warm from racks of overhead can lights.

*Showtime.* Before he had gone ten feet, he whipped off his leather jacket and tossed it to her. She caught it by reflex.

"Thanks, babe." He hung his hands on his waist, giving everyone an eyeful of "rock star" while he surveyed the studio. "It's hotter than hell in here. I'll need some Lauquen. Can't work when I'm dehydrated."

"What?" She held his coat well away from her, her hackles rising.

"*Lau-quen?* Designer water? Ring any bells?" He pointed at the lights. "And some of this wattage has got to go." He caught Stan trying to make for the door. "It's in all my contracts. Tell 'em, Stan." As Stan muttered a confirmation, she tossed the coat aside and struggled with her temper. She was hot? He smiled. She was going to get even hotter.

"First of all, my name is Samantha Drexel, not *Babe*," she bit out in those husky tones that made his fingertips vibrate. "I am the marketing manager who came up with the idea of using your music in our valentines. It was someone else's bright idea to issue a full CD of your songs, and we're having to 'crash' production. So if you don't mind—"

Nick whirled on Stan. "A CD? You let BMR sell them full tracks?"

Stan mouthed the words *money, money, money* as he rubbed his thumb and fingers together and ducked out the door. It was all Nick could do not to charge after him and throttle the old rat bastard until his hairpiece went flying. They were reissuing his old stuff!

For a minute he grappled for control. For the past six years he'd labored in small clubs and worked endless studio sessions and jazz festivals, trying to bury his hard rocking reputation and forge a new identity for himself and his music. Then an ambitious corporate climber gets a bright idea and all his hard work goes down the tubes. He stared at her.

She was so going to regret that creative impulse.

"Lauquen comes from a special artesian aquifer in Argentina." He gestured to his throat. "The trace manganese in the water coats the pipes."

"Which is irrelevant, since you will just be posing," she declared, stalking over to confront him.

"I don't *pose*, Brunhilda, I *sing*. You have a sound system in this place, I assume. And my tracks." He leaned close enough to read the odd blend of resentment and expectation in her eyes. Striking golden eyes. Narrowing dangerously. *"Then let's do it."*

# 2

SAM STOOD WITH HER hands on her waist, mirroring his pose, trying to maintain an upright-and-locked position. He was inches away, filling her vision, making her heart jackhammer and her knees go weak.

She couldn't swallow.

*Nick Stack.* Wearing his trademark black jeans and shirt—open to that critical fourth button—and black Italian boots. Six feet three inches of free-range testosterone, with prominent cheekbones and fabulous teeth. He seemed leaner than he had been back in the day, but somehow he came across as all the more defined for it…as if the ease and artifice had been stripped away to reveal the raw essence of the man underneath. Twelve years after his hard-rocking heyday, he exuded a tested but still defiant sexuality that dared women to look. And touch.

She curled her hands into fists at her sides.

She had enough trouble with his cursed music. Having to resist both it and him at close range—she sucked a sharp breath.

*Focus, damn it.* She was here to see he fulfilled his contract. This was business, not pleasure.

Stepping back, she looked for photographer Halcyon White. He stood nearby with his assistant, watching them in a very intent way.

"Where's the stereo?" she asked, grateful she didn't sound choked.

When he directed her to a rack of electronic equipment on the back wall, she pulled out her cell phone and headed for the system controls.

"It's me," she said when Renee answered in their offices, above, on the thirty-eighth floor. "Find that CD of Stack's and bring it down… fast."

"He's there?" Renee asked, perking up. "He made it this time?"

"In the flesh," Sam said, regretting that choice of words the instant she clicked off. *Flesh.* Suffering a brief shiver, she made herself focus and located the receiver, disk tray and output controls.

When she returned, Stack had sent an assistant running for his pricey water and was sorting through the backdrop choices, declaring them to be "crap." She clamped her jaw and headed for him, but Halcyon—living up to his name—grabbed her by the elbow and shook his head.

"I look best in grays and white lights with a hint of ultra-violet," Stack declared, seizing a glaring white backdrop. "This'll do."

"Brilliant," Halcyon declared, strolling over to him, seeming oddly relaxed. "If you're going for a vampire-in-the-morning look."

"It works for me," Stack said with a fierce smile.

Halcyon chuckled.

"I think we need a warmer background to showcase you," he said in measured tones. His own handsome chocolate skin and winter-white ensemble were such a statement that it was hard to argue with his eye for the subtleties of lighting on a human form. "This is going on a CD cover as well as a POS poster surrounded by valentine reds."

"*P-O-S?*" Nick said, frowning.

"Point of sale." Sam crossed her arms. "You're going to

be hanging in four thousand corporate stores, nation-wide...with feature space in another five thousand outlets that carry CrownCraft goods...surrounded by flocked red velvet and fuzzy teddy bears and pictures of swans with their necks entwined to form hearts."

She couldn't tell—did the news cause that blanch or was he just making another bid for his vampire lighting scheme?

"I'll need a mike," he said to Halcyon's assistant, his jaw flexing. "Doesn't have to be live, but I always use one." He spotted and headed for the makeup table. The fortysomething makeup technician looked positively orgasmic as he slid into her chair and winked at her.

Sam made herself look away. He still had it, all right.

When Halcyon called that he was ready, Stack sprang up from the chair, took a swig of his expensive water and grabbed the prop mike. She had Renee punch the sound system and braced as the riveting, bass-heavy introduction of "Baby, Tonight" went rumbling through the studio.

They all watched, growing spellbound as he did a few deft slides, steps and hip thrusts that carried him through the opening bars.

"A man that tall shouldn't be able to move like that," Renee said from beside her, sounding a little breathless.

Sam shivered and clamped her arms fiercely around herself. Between Stack's aphrodisiacal music and eye-popping exhibitionism...she had to get out of there...maybe slip upstairs to her office...

She took two steps backward, tripped on a fat power cable and nearly went down on her rear. Her flailing caught Stack's eye.

He halted and the recording went on without him, sounding thin.

"This isn't working," he declared. "I don't just sing, I sing to an audience." He glanced around the studio. Before anyone could point out that there were half a dozen assistants standing around, he fixed on Sam.

"Brunhilda. Come on down." He made for her.

"I have work to do. My assistant can—"

"This was *your* idea, right?" He grabbed her by the wrist and snagged a stool as he headed for the backdrop. "See it through."

"This is absurd," she growled, trying frantically to pull back.

"Actually it's not." Halcyon appeared at her elbow to usher her toward the stool. "It will give him a focus and keep his energy up."

"I don't want to—" *keep anything of his* up "—be in these photos," she said, digging in her spike heels.

"Just sit still and keep your hands to yourself," Halcyon said with a chuckle. "I'll shoot around you."

It was a nightmare; she was stuck on a stool under hot studio lights with Stack bombarding her with provocative lyrics while pictures were snapped all around her. She hung her heels over the top rung of the stool and tucked her arms tightly, trying to make herself a smaller target.

*Just an hour or so,* she told herself frantically. *Ignore the heat. And the beat. And for God's sake keep your knees together.*

Then Stack put the mike to his mouth and began to belt out lyrics.

*Ohhh.*

*Damn.*

At point-blank range, his voice was deep and full of earthy undertones and had an edge of raw half-pained pleasure not unlike the burn of hot chilies sliding down her throat. The sound seeped into her blood and co-opted her heartbeat, replacing it with a steady quarter-time rhythm. Her exposed skin went taut and began to vibrate as if it were a drum head, and she trembled as he crooned about how he wanted to make love to her until he couldn't tell her body from his own.

He moved in, swaying, undulating as he ground out the raw, erotic invitation that had made him famous.

She looked away, but he danced himself in front of her, filling her vision and dragging her gaze toward his. It took heroic effort, but she swiveled on the stool, giving him her side and shoulder. There was a tug at the back of her head and she felt her hair slide out of her ponytail. Shocked, she reached up to feel her shoulder-length hair hanging free.

"Loosen up, 'Hilda." He tossed the elastic band in her lap.

It was a small but telling encroachment, a declaration that nothing—not even her person—was out of bounds where this man was concerned. Stiffening with panic, she sent him her hottest glare and prayed he couldn't tell how the liberty he'd just taken affected her.

As the serenade continued, her legs ached with erotic tension and sweat droplets trickled down the side of her face and between her breasts.

"Getting hot, are you?" Stack gave her a wink.

Flirting? More like taunting, she thought, fanning herself with the sides of the jacket she was afraid to shed. Her nipples stuck out like hood ornaments beneath her thin sleeveless sweater.

Looking from Halcyon to Renee and the rest of the crew—all watching eagerly—she felt her face flame, lowered her feet and tried not to squirm on the stool. She had to gut this out.

Another song came and went, and then came one that was slower and more evocative, a steamy ballad she knew well and had been dreading.

Halfway through, she was jarred by the feel of her jacket sliding from her shoulders. She was shocked to have Halcyon direct his assistant to take it from Stack. She had apparently drifted into a memory-upholstered lull.

A shudder rippled through her as she folded her arms to cover her breasts. The Stackman went down on one knee beside her, engulfing her with his seductive presence and suggestive words. Then he pulled her gaze into his…ran a hand over her shoulder…massaged his way down her spine. Could he feel her body trembling?

She swayed, gripping the edges of the seat, wishing she could give him a shove to back him off, but Halcyon was in close now, working furiously. The camera was whirring and snapping just over her shoulder.

She closed her eyes and began to repeat the words to "The Star-Spangled Banner" over and over in her head. When the barrage of sensation ended, she opened her eyes and found Stack looming over her with a smug twist of a smile. What was he…? She froze.

Something wasn't quite. Her breasts felt…*loose*. The memory of his hand moving down her back suddenly made a very different kind of sense. Her face caught fire as the re-alization hit.

*The son of a bitch had unfastened her bra!*

Her heart pounded in her throat as she exploded off the stool, grabbed him by the elbow and yanked him around to face her. He was grinning broadly now, watching her realize what he'd done and enjoying the way her D cups were riding up beneath her thin knit sweater. She clamped her other arm under her breasts.

"I need a word with you, Mr. Stack. *Now!*" She hauled him out the doors and into the hall. But the staff and crew collected in the doorway, so she pulled him down the hall…where the floor receptionist stared at them.

Apparently the only place she could have this out with him unobserved was the damned elevator! When she shoved the button, the door miraculously opened. She hauled him inside and hit the stop button as they started down.

Turning her back to him, she pulled up her sweater to bare her dangling bra hooks.

"You undid it, you *fix* it. You're not getting out of this elevator until you do."

"Promises, promises," he said with a laugh. "You sure you don't want to just take it the rest of the way off?"

She shot him a fierce look over her shoulder.

*"Fasten it."*

After a nerve-racking pause, he refastened the hooks.

She dropped her sweater back in place and whirled on him.

"Look, you've made it abundantly clear you don't want to be here." She jammed her fists on her hips. "News flash— I'm not crazy about you being here either. But if you think a little personal harassment is going to get you out of your contractual obligations, you're badly mistaken."

His sardonic smile disappeared.

Three months of anger and humiliation came boiling up in her.

She raised her chin and stalked closer, sending him back a step.

"This line is too important to fail because of one asshole's ego."

He backed another step, and she advanced again.

"Whether you realize it or not, people's jobs and homes and families are on the line, here. Designers, sound engineers, photographers, production line personnel, wholesalers, retailers, promoters in three cities, merchants in the malls you'll appear in… In the worst economy in decades, we've sunk a million dollars in development costs and hundreds of design hours into producing musical cards, a CD and posters that feature your face and your signature sounds. Not to mention the slice *you* took right out of the middle of the pie.

"This has to work. I'm not going to let it fail, you hear

me?" She punched his chest with a finger. "I am not laying off my people and watching them sink into foreclosure beca-ause—" she had to force out the last part after her voice broke "—because you insist on acting like a horny, out-of-control fifteen-year-old!"

# 3

NICK WATCHED SAMANTHA Drexel struggle visibly for control. In the midst of backing him into a corner and dressing him down, emotion got the better of her and tears suddenly welled in her eyes. He could see they horrified her. She stiffened, jerked back and flipped the elevator switch to start the car.

Tears. She was angry. And hurt.

And *human*.

Fiery emotions simmered beneath that daunting corporate cool.

He suddenly had that damned feeling in his chest again—a sliding, sinking sensation that left him feeling confused and guilty for acting like a total asshole in order to get out of obligations he'd entered into freely. He'd taken the Crown-Craft money with both hands, feeling justified in thinking it came from some greedy, soulless corporation. But after two minutes in an elevator with Samantha Drexel—who accused him of that very same greed and indifference—he was knocked on his ass by how self-serving his assumptions were. What made him think that the people in companies were any less human or deserving of honorable dealings than he was?

She stood with her back to him, her nose practically pressed against the elevator doors in her eagerness to escape. He watched her swipe at her cheeks and had an overpowering urge to reach out to her…to touch her…to pull her into his arms…to *hold* her. Stunned and more than a little alarmed by those unprecedented impulses, he stayed where he was, leaning against the wall, trying to figure out what was happening to him.

The instant the doors opened, she charged off. He watched the doors close, battling the urge to go after her, until the elevator, summoned by someone on a level below, started down again.

SAM WAS TOO OVERWROUGHT, too confused by her own feelings to pay attention to whether or not he exited behind her. All she could focus on was putting some distance between herself and Nicholas Stack. What she couldn't escape, however, was the shocking feeling of being fully alive, of running on all cylinders for the first time in weeks. Despite or because of that humiliating lapse into tears, she felt purged and cleared of the emotional garbage that had been weighing her down.

By the time she reached the studio, she felt so much better. Apparently yelling at one man was as therapeutic as yelling at another.

Several minutes later, just as she was starting to think that she'd really blown it, Stack rolled through the door. His intensity was still there, but his attitude was all business as he approached Halcyon.

When he stepped onto the backdrop again, it was with an acoustic guitar from the prop closet. He asked that the canned music be stopped and then stood with his head back and eyes closed for a moment, gathering himself. There was a deepening silence as he tightened the strings and then began to run a melody line, tapping instead of plucking or strumming. The effect made it sound as if two or three musicians were playing.

He paused long enough to beckon to her. She had no idea what he was up to, but some small, indefinable change in him undercut her refusal. That, and her own curiosity. She hesitated long enough for all to see that compliance with his request was her decision.

When she was settled back on the stool and he started to play, her toes curled inside the classic black Louboutin stilettos she had worn for a boost of playing-in-the-big-leagues confidence.

The lights dimmed and a spotlight appeared out of nowhere. He propped a foot on the rungs of her stool, rested the guitar on his leg and began to coax sounds from the instrument that seemed as if they came from a whole ensemble. It was a potent and utterly unique sound, laced through with Nick Stack's sensual magic. When he paused to turn her chin so she would look at him, she allowed it, and those big silver-gray eyes of his caused the bottom to fall out of her stomach.

Studio and audience slowly melted away, leaving only a circle of light in a sea of darkness, inhabited by two. Nick Stack was there with her, serenading her in a different, jazz-like sound, singing about how he wanted her…making her want him.

Something snapped inside her, releasing desires she had hoarded for years. Need unfolded deep in her body and sent tendrils of desire curling around every nerve she possessed. She felt her body going taut, ripening with anticipation as she looked up into his chiseled face.

For one breathtaking moment she glimpsed what true passion felt like. A real, soul-jarring, life-changing need.

Her skin burned where his fingertips had connected with it. The electricity between them settled into a steady, sinuous alternating current that powered the sexy images rolling through her inner senses. All she could think was that she wished he'd stop singing and kiss her. She wanted those lips. That beautiful, decadent mouth. She felt herself gravitating closer, leaning, just inches away…

The music ended, the lights came up and she looked around in dismay at being rudely jarred from that delicious and compelling reverie.

Stack pulled back and set the guitar aside, but she couldn't seem to move. She felt *melted* from the center out. A veritable puddle.

Applause broke out from the back, near the door, and he gave a stage bow in that direction. She seized the moment to collect herself, slide off the stool and wobble over to grab her jacket.

She only half heard Halcyon say that he'd gotten some fantastic shots and would see that Nick got proofs, and she vaguely noticed the way people collected around Stack for autographs for "nieces" and "nephews." All she could focus on was him. She stared at his profile…nose just large enough to keep his face from being pretty…sleek cheekbones, squared chin, long lashes, that bold, sexy mouth…

Half of her was snarling *snap out of it* and the other half was purring like a well-tuned Ferrari.

The big overhead can lights went off, plunging the studio into relative gloom, and she looked up to find Stack coming toward her with his jacket slung over a shoulder. Caught between wanting to take a step back and being tempted to step directly into his path, she avoided both by heading for the doors.

"I need a ride back to the hotel." He caught up with her and kept pace.

"It's just a few blocks away. The walk will do you good." She couldn't resist looking at him from the corner of her eye. There was a sheen of moisture on his skin, and his tousled hair looked slightly damp. *Have mercy.* Even filtered through her defenses he was an overwhelming package. "It'll give you a chance to cool off."

Again the elevator miracle; the doors opened right away and she stepped in and hit the up button. He followed, and seconds later she was alone in that space with him again, stopped halfway between floors.

Only, he had pushed the stop button this time.

She looked up, feeling her every nerve go on alert as he moved in close, and she gripped the sides of her jacket as if it were a life preserver.

"What do you think you're doing?"

He had no idea. He just knew that this was more than some appetite that had tagged along with the rock-star persona he'd dredged up. The way she had looked up at him while he was singing, the hunger and promise and challenge in her eyes, he didn't intend to let Samantha Drexel get away before he had chance to figure it out.

"I'm not the asshole you think I am," he blurted out, bracing an arm against the elevator wall beside her.

"As my old granny used to say—" she lifted her chin and her voice dropped a third "'—asshole is as asshole does.'"

"You must have one hell of an old granny."

"You have no idea." Those husky tones rattled through him, sliding down the skin of his belly, tantalizing that sensitive territory.

"Not true." He lowered his gaze to her chest and then brought it slowly back up to her eyes, appreciating every square centimeter between. She was a handful. *"I have plenty of ideas."*

And the idea battering his self-control at that moment involved him lowering his parted lips over hers and pulling her hard against his body. He didn't have a choice, really. He couldn't *not* kiss her.

The instant their mouths made contact, a surge of energy

rushed through him that momentarily blanked awareness of everything but the warmth and resilience of her lips. He wasn't aware they were moving until she hit the nearby elevator wall with a soft thud.

His eyes popped open to find her staring at him, seeming a little shocked. Had he misread the way she had looked at him while he was sing— *Damn, her lips were soft.* When her mouth moved, it took him a minute to realize she was speaking, not kissing.

"Being a great kisser doesn't mean you can't be a jerk, too." The vibrations of her husky whisper set his lips, his whole face tingling.

"It *was* pretty great, wasn't it? I've wanted to do that since the minute I heard your voice. Has anybody ever told you that you sound like—"

"Lauren Bacall with a chest cold?" she said against his mouth.

"Exactly." He pulled his chin back to appreciate her flushed face.

She looked into his eyes with an expression that teetered between astonishment and disbelief, but she didn't exactly seem eager to escape.

"Has anybody ever said *no* to you in your entire life?"

"Lots of people. In fact, music execs seem to really get off on it."

"Yeah, well, they must not be female," she muttered, staring at his mouth and seeming a bit startled that she'd spoken aloud.

With a rumble of amusement he bent to kiss her again, and she lifted her chin to meet him. A tidal wave of heat crashed through him. He suddenly wanted to see Samantha Drexel's passions break free, to make them break free, in his arms, under his naked body.

Her mouth responded, molding intimately to his as her body sank against him—breasts, abdomen, pelvis, thighs—

centimeter by delicious centimeter. By the time her anatomy was introduced fully to his, it was all he could do to stand upright and kiss at the same time. He sucked an air-starved breath. *Damn*. It felt as if his eyes were crossed!

She leaned to the side and he dropped his arm to let her reach the controls. There was a hum and a lurch as the car started moving again.

When she looked up, her eyes were so warm—big, distracting amber disks with brighter golden rings around their desire-darkened centers. Her face was flushed and her lips were kiss-swollen perfection.

"Let me buy you a drink, Samantha Drexel," he said, his voice now almost as husky as hers. "Give me a chance to explain."

She searched his eyes even as he searched hers, and he couldn't help wondering what she saw. A has-been trying to skate through life on past glories? An aging stud eager to make one more conquest for ego's sake?

"Don't say no." He held his breath, willing those guarded golden eyes to concede, unsettled by how much her answer mattered to him.

The elevator opened to reveal a group of people standing just outside in animated conversation…including Samantha Drexel's assistant, whose jaw dropped at the sight of her boss being pressed like a panini between the elevator wall and Nick's overheated body. As the doors closed, an older guy with a graying ponytail leaned along with it to get a better look and burst into a wicked grin.

He felt as much as heard Sam's groan.

"You'd better make that drink a double."

# 4

THE DRAKE WAS THE CLASSIEST, most elegant hotel in town, the place famous politicos and Hollywood royalty stayed when they hit Chicago. Doormen, marble, polished brass and lush carpets…right now it all made Sam feel as if she should be wearing a big scarlet *S* on her chest. *S* for *sin*. Or *spectacular,* which was undoubtedly what a night with the Prince of Give-It-Up-Baybee would be, if that kiss were any indication. Not that he'd said anything about a night, or about sin either, for that matter.

But she had watched his body move as they exited the cab and thought of how he would look naked and hard, muscles pumped, braced above her. And as they entered the lobby, she couldn't take her eyes off the flexing of his long, muscular legs beneath those worn jeans and the rhythmic sway of his shoulders. Sex was exactly where this was headed; the certainty unrolled in her like a roadmap.

It was insane. Her sinking inhibitions were clearly pulling her principles down with them. Getting physical with Nick would only compound her mixing-business-and-pleasure issues. On the other hand, she could just hear Tori and Kitty reacting to the news that she'd passed up a mind-blowing bout of pleasure and walked away from a lifelong dream.

*Girl, your manhunting license ought to be revoked.*

Hell, it was going to be revoked anyway when she came up dateless on Valentine's Day. So why not enjoy the *now?*

Her body came alive with anticipation as they passed on the elegant Palm Court where high tea was in progress and opted for the lobby bar instead. By the time he slid into the leather-clad banquette beside her, she had gooseflesh all over her legs and was so tense with suppressed arousal that she practically snapped "gin and tonic" at the waiter.

"You were going to explain?" she said, trying to pull her gaze from his moist, parted lips. Finding that impossible, she focused instead on trying to control her breathing. It was probably bad form to pant all over your girlhood sex god.

He slid an arm along the back of the banquette and leaned in.

"I didn't want to do the shoot," he said, "because I knew it would be all about my old songs and that's not my sound anymore. I haven't been a rocker in a long time. I've moved on from all of that. I'm a different man, with different music."

"You seem pretty 'Nick Stack' to me." Swallowing, she gave up fighting the pull of his magnetism and let it drag her closer. "Sound like him, too." She licked her lower lip. "Except…maybe, better."

"Better?" His mouth drew up on one side, into the most decadent expression she'd ever seen. "How's that?"

"Fuller. Earthier. More complex." She squeezed her thighs together to quell the burning ignited between them. "Just more *you.*"

"More *me?* You mean, like that last song?"

"Especially that last song." Her face flamed—from his breath curling over her skin or the memory of what that song had done to her?

"That was my new sound, my *real* sound. I've worked long and hard develop a whole different voice in jazz, and I'm trying to cut a new record deal. Rereleasing that old schlock will only confuse things."

"I don't think anyone will be the least bit confused," she

said, her throat tight and her tongue—its mind clearly on another duty—a little clumsy. "They'll hear Nick Stack's rough velvet tones and think—"

"Yeah? What will they think?"

His mouth grazed hers, shunting thought onto a sensual side track.

"What I always think when I hear your voice."

"Which is?"

"'Do me right,'" she quoted his lyrics, shocked to hear it come so bluntly out of her mouth. "'Tonight.'"

*Sweet Jesus.* Had she just propositioned him?

Then he supplied the next line, pouring it between her tingling lips.

"'Yeah, bay-bee.'"

That unabashedly erotic refrain, half spoken, half sung in the deepest, sexiest part of his range, turned her blood to syrup. The bar, the other patrons, the upscale, old-school propriety of the place—suddenly nothing mattered but her desire for the feel and taste of him.

As their lips collided, the lightning that was produced shattered all the inhibitions holding her back. Her hands flew to his hair; his sank around her waist. She pressed closer, wanting every solid, sexy inch of him against every aching, hungry inch of her.

Pleasure seared down the back of her throat like a triple shot of single malt, leaving in its wake only a half-coherent vow that she would not regret whatever came next. This was a once-in-a-lifetime opportunity. A dream come true.

She ran her hands down his neck and shoulders to biceps that were flexed hard and filled with the same tension she was feeling…just as the waiter arrived with their drinks and gave a muffled cough that could have been either disapproval or recognition.

They broke apart and Nick slid to the edge of the booth,

tossing some bills onto the table beside the untouched drinks and pulling her along.

The elevator doors opened the very instant he pressed the button. It was no surprise that the minute the doors closed, he pressed her back against the wall and kissed her until vertigo set in. She was oxygen deprived and panting as if she'd just finished the Boston Marathon by the time a discreet ding announced they had arrived on the tenth floor.

The elevator doors were closing again before he reached out to stop them and pulled her out into the hall. Whipping out a key card, he led her past several rooms to a pair of ornate doors bearing a classy suite name.

"We paid for this?" She glanced around a parlor furnished with a baby grand piano, a full-size bar, and ultra-plush sofas that probably cost more than her car.

"Habit. From the old days," he said, ripping off his jacket. "Demand the best and you get treated like the best. Record label logic."

"That actually works?" She watched the way his shoulders flexed and his shirt tightened across his lean muscles. *Have mercy.* She could die on the spot, this minute, and consider her life fulfilled.

"Today," he said, prowling toward her with an appreciative look that made her flush with pleasure. "Today it's working just fine."

A heartbeat later he was kissing her witless and she was running her hands possessively over those memorable shoulders and up that broad back. His kisses were long, lush and lubricating enough to free all the rusty impulses she had refused to exercise ever again until it was right.

And, baby, this was *right.*

Her legs trembled and her intimate muscles clenched as he peeled off her jacket. Her skirt stayed in place, caught between their straining bodies, until he gave a wicked laugh and backed off enough to let it fall. She fumbled with his shirt buttons but soon was kissing her way down a slice of bared skin. He tasted of salt and a sharp, clean tang of arousal. She was suddenly starving for more.

"Briefs," she whispered as she sank her hands between his jeans and his tight, muscular buttocks. "I would have guessed commando."

"Overrated," he murmured as his mouth migrated down the side of her face and neck to her shoulder. "Zipper rash." Then while nuzzling her throat, he gave the back panel of her bra a tug. "Undo it." When she met his gaze, there was an odd glint in his eye. "After today, I'm not going anywhere I'm not invited." His voice dropped to a whisper and his eyelids lowered to produce a very focused smolder. "So invite me."

That multilayered request tugged her heart wide open. It was now or never, all or nothing. She dropped her bra and held her breath. His appreciative groan sent a shiver of exultation through her. His fingers closed around her breasts as if they were national treasures.

When he bent to rake her sensitized nipples with his tongue, her knees gave. Laughing with a wicked edge, he wrapped his arms around her naked waist and hauled her up onto her toes, against him. Every tug of his mouth at her breasts sent a sweet spear of arousal straight to her sex.

They stumbled through the bedroom door, still joined, and sank together onto the bed…knees first, then hips, elbows and shoulders. She shivered as he rolled her onto her back, nipping her breasts and running his hands up her bare sides, giving extra attention to every part that made her breath catch.

Skin against glorious skin and stroke upon quivering stroke…sensation poured through her in torrents. He shifted to the side, nibbling his way down her body. Her every muscle—even her lungs—contracted when his fingers began to strum her slick, swollen flesh and jacked her response to a whole new level.

She pulled his mouth up to hers and pressed wantonly against those fingers, urging them inside her, seeking what they could give—needing, demanding, breathless—until her nerves shorted, muscles seized and reality blurred.

For a moment she floated out of body—expanded, freed—before sinking back into a steamy haze of need.

"Now, Nick—" She reached for him.

He sucked in a sharp breath and his hand closed around her wrist.

"Give me a minute, babe." He rolled to the side and the sound of the foil ripping brought her halfway back to reality. "Like the song says—" he gave her a wink "—there's nothin' like 'a sharp-dressed man.'"

That unexpected thoughtfulness gave her a glimpse of the man behind the public guise, a man who kept one foot firmly on the ground even when his hormones were leaving planet Earth behind. As she brushed his hands away, taking the condom and rolling it down the length of him, his eyes went molten and he turned to ribbed steel beneath her hands.

With a growl, he pulled her beneath him and settled purposefully between her legs. The weight of him, the feel of his body blanketing her, his heat molding her, turned her breath to gasps.

Pleasure saturated her as he raked her sex with his, pausing along the way, tantalizing her with the hint of fulfilling her desire. Then he pressed slowly, centimeter by delicious centimeter into her, parting her, filling her to heart-stopping perfection. He moved so rhythmically, drawing her to meet each stroke, to luxuriate in the feel of being penetrated, filled and claimed, to seek that elusive blend of position and pressure that would bring release.

"Samantha," he muttered, adjusting each movement until he found the precise angle and thrust that wrung helpless shudders of response from her. "Samantha…Samantha…Samantha…"

She crashed through every sensory boundary, shattering. When her thoughts reassembled and her vision returned, she was holding him fiercely while aftershocks of pleasure rumbled through them both. He finally slid to the bed beside her, murmuring her name over and over as if trying to brand each sensation with her identity.

When she turned to him a moment later, he was watching her with a soft smile.

"Wow," she said. "You're really, really good at this."

"Practice makes perfect," he said, his smile dimming.

"Then you must have practiced a lot." It was said lightly, but as his gaze clouded, she wished she could take it back.

"That's how rock legends are made, and there was a time I wanted to—" He paused to meet her gaze. "I won't lie to you, Sam. There were lots of women. That's just part of the package with me. Somehow I managed to make it through that stuff healthy and relatively sane. So I have no desire to be a legend anymore. It's enough for me to be a good musician and songwriter. And someday, hopefully, a good man."

He pulled her into the curve of his body and nuzzled her neck. She sighed and welcomed that honesty into her soul.

A good man. Now, there was a concept.

And at that moment she thought he didn't have far to go.

## 5

SHE AWOKE SOME TIME later to a quiet, darkened bedroom, feeling as if she'd just finished a triathlon and come in *first*. For every ache, there was a stunningly thorough sense of satisfaction to compensate. The bed beside her was empty and she sat up, registering a slice of light coming from the mostly closed sitting-room door. Soft strains of music reached her.

Nick? At the piano? His statement that he was a different man with different music suddenly took on a larger meaning. He expressed himself through music. If he felt anything like she did just now, making music was the very place he'd go.

Spotting a hotel robe flung across a nearby chair, she snagged it and headed for the bathroom. The warm spray of the shower felt wonderful, and by the time she donned the fluffy robe again, she felt ready to face him.

He was indeed at the piano when she padded barefoot into the parlor. Halfway across the sitting room, she was stopped in her tracks by a dreamy piano concerto. Liszt? Mozart? Schumann? One of those classical guys. Nick was playing with his eyes closed, totally absorbed, looking as if every note resounded in his soul.

As she listened, he began to vary the tempo and emphasis of certain phrases, giving them a more contemporary sound. The transition to another style was seamless, natural, almost effortless. Drawn to this glimpse of him in the grip of a very different passion, she moved silently to the piano and watched as he transitioned back to the classical mode.

Her concept of him changed yet again. He was a true musician. This wasn't garage band stuff; this took training and discipline as much as desire. And to be able to shift so easily, so creatively between styles…

He was a man of unexpected depths. Just seeing him like this, soul-bared, expressing himself honestly, joyfully in music, was enough to topple the rest of her defenses. In that moment, she felt a connection to him unlike any she'd felt to a man before. It seemed like her entire life had been preparing her for this moment. Nothing had ever seemed so right.

NICK OPENED HIS EYES and was startled by the sight of Samantha leaning on the piano, her eyes luminous with wonder. He had pulled on jeans before heading to the piano, but at that moment he felt more than naked; he felt exposed in a way that made every nerve in his body go strangely quiet. Claiming that inner calm, he focused on her flushed cheeks and tousled hair. In her eyes he saw warmth, acceptance, recognition. She liked what she saw and heard. He relaxed in a way he'd never experienced with a woman.

"You didn't learn that from old Eric Clapton albums," she said.

"Juilliard." He ran a complex finger exercise up and down the keyboard to demonstrate. "For a while. Until I fell in with bad company."

"Rockers?" She leaned her elbows on the piano top.

"Guitars." He chuckled. "My piano teacher was horrified."

"How did we not hear that you were a 'serious' musician?"

"When you're a Top Forty rocker, you don't exactly want

that kind of stuff getting around. It ruins the fast-and-loose image."

"So you're a classically trained musician who pitched the 'purity of art' for commercial success," she said.

"Guilty as charged." He launched into a jazz improvisation. "It was all fun and fame games at first. Then I got bored and felt trapped and tried to do something more original." He felt a reflex tightening in his gut at the recall of old battles, but forced it to relax again.

"But it didn't work," she concluded for him.

*Perceptive woman.*

"I got taken to school about the reality of the music business." He paused in the middle of a promising melody line. "And I found out I still had a hell of a lot to learn, about music, about myself."

"So that's why you haven't recorded for a while?"

"It would be easy to say yes." He took a deep breath, wondering if she would understand. "But the truth is, nobody wanted anything from me but the old pop-rock schlock. I doubt they even want that anymore."

"Hey." She scowled. "A lot of people loved that 'schlock.'"

"Yeah. Pimple-faced adolescents, dance-club studs and hard-bangin' groupies." Sarcasm crept in. "Quite a stellar musical legacy—'helping frat boys get laid since 1996.' *Now available in sound bites—*" his voice went TV-announcer resonant "*—coming to a valentine near you.*"

"That's a little harsh," she said, caught between a smile and a scowl.

"Yeah? How would you feel, if your best days were chopped up to use as punchlines in valentines?" The question came out harsher than he had intended.

"My best work *is* the punchlines of valentines." He tensed, his hands still on the keys until she smiled. "But I see your point. Put that way, it doesn't exactly sound flattering." She slid around the piano and looked at him with genuine warmth.

"But you need to know, Nick, that we chose your music, your signature lines and phrases, because people recognize them instantly and love to hear them." She paused for a breath. "*I* love to hear them."

The glow in her eyes registered "sincerity," causing his heart to trip.

"You were a fan back in the day?" he said, conjuring an image of a nubile young Samantha Drexel in a schoolgirl uniform, gyrating to his sexed-up music. His whole body snapped taut.

"I slept beneath a poster of you on my dorm wall at Cornell," she said. "Almost lost my virginity on the dance floor to 'Make Me Yours.'"

"You and half the teenage girls in North America." He shook his head. "It's a wonder I wasn't stoned by village elders after each concert."

When he looked up, her expression was so unguarded, so earnest that he could actually *see* the young girl she had been. If only he had—no, if he'd met her then, she might have been just one more honey, one more anonymous night in a monotonous string of hotel rooms. He traced her cheek with his knuckles. Now she was more. But how much more?

"A lot of people fell in love to your music, you know. Including me." She nodded ruefully. "Twice. With the same damned guy."

"Same *damned* guy?" His gaze flew to her bare ring finger and he felt a slide of relief. "He's not still around?"

"No. Thank heaven. It was a college romance that I thought deserved a second chance." There was a hint of pain in her face. "Turned out I was wrong."

"Thank heaven," he echoed, making room for her and patting the bench beside him.

"Play me something," she said, tucking her feet primly under the bench, then laying a hand on his upper thigh. "One of your new songs. I want to hear more of the *evolved* you. The real Nicholas Stack."

"Okay. But I should warn you that your hand—" he glanced at the supple fingers splayed across his leg "—is very near my restart button."

She leaned into his shoulder while purposefully tightening her grip on his thigh. "And your hands on those keys are near mine. *Play.*"

With a sound that was part growl, part chuckle, he began to play, demonstrating the differences between his old sound and what he was doing now. Jazz was more fluid and free-form, he told her, then proceeded to show her how his megahit "Baby Tonight" could have an entirely different impact when done in that style.

At the end of the song she looked up in amazement.

"That's what you want to do now?" She sounded as if she'd been holding her breath. When he nodded, she ran her hand down his arm and caressed his fingers. "That's amazing! Why aren't they following you around recording and releasing every blessed note you play?"

He chuckled. "Good question."

*"More."* Her eyes shone. "Play some more."

Savoring the excitement in her face, he warned that the next song was a work in progress, then began to unspool a provocative jazz number that had always made him think of a woman's body swaying in invitation. She melted against him; he could feel her tensing and relaxing, responding viscerally at all the right places. She apparently experienced music with her whole body.

He understood that kind of connection. It was the way he immersed himself in his music and experienced it with every part of his being. He closed his eyes, willing the song to touch and move her, wanting to share with her what he felt when he created it.

"No lyrics?" she whispered dryly, her hand tightening on his thigh.

"Not yet." He poured the passion rising in him through the instrument, caressing the keys the way he yearned to touch her lush body.

"It's wonderful." She laid a cheek against his shoulder. "It's like you've captured a heartbeat. Mine. You could call it 'Variations on Samantha Drexel's Heartbeat.' Play it again."

When she rose to stand behind him, he canted his head while he played and was rewarded with nibbles up his neck to his ear. Shivers shot down his spine as she circled him with her arms and ran her hands over his shoulders and bare chest, exploring him.

The soft prickle of the terry robe against his back gave way to something sleeker, warmer and softer. Breasts? Was she— She was rubbing hers against him! His arousal went from zero to sixty as he both felt and glimpsed the robe falling to the floor. He would have stopped in the middle of the song, but she bent and ordered huskily in his ear, "Keep playing…if you want me to keep playing."

Peeling open her robe, she dragged the tips of her naked breasts against his bare shoulders, soothing and stimulating her nipples at the same time. She swayed with the music, pressing softer and harder as the music rose and fell. As that sensual ache spread through the rest of her, she dropped the robe altogether and pressed her body against him, undulating against his broad back, tantalizing him.

His hands stilled on the keys. She raised her head enough to ask "Want me to stop?" before raking her teeth over his throbbing pulse.

Watching the way his body tensed and flexed in response

to her provocative actions, she sank to the floor on her knees behind him, circling his waist with her arms and working the snap and zipper of his jeans. He *was* commando this time. His penis came free, filling her hands, and he rocked against her grip, thrusting into the pressure of her palms. He managed only a few more bars before pulling her up and across his lap.

"You are, without a doubt, the best audience I've ever had." His voice was ragged with need as his gaze settled on her breasts. "Those are downright magnificent, sweetheart. I'm gonna see them in my dreams."

She pushed to her knees on the bench and slid a leg across his lap, bringing her chest level with his eyes.

"Knock yourself out, Stackman." She arched her shoulders to emphasize the offer. "They're all yours." He seemed frozen, so she cupped one breast and thrust it higher, offering it to him. With a groan, he fastened on it and sucked sharply, sending raw pleasure streaking to her sex again. She shuddered and began to slide her wet heat up and down his erection.

His head came up, lips glistening, eyes dark and luminous.

"Pocket—" he rasped, trembling as he searched for the opening.

She shifted her leg, ran her hand down the fabric until she found the condom. She pulled it out and pressed it into his palm.

"You do it," she said against his lips, "I'm busy."

Seconds later his hands were on her hips, guiding her down onto him. The angle was perfect, the contact was intense, and it didn't take long for both of them to see stars. And skyrockets. And colliding planets. It was a whole damned NASA launch of sexual release.

Even more remarkable was the *afterglow*. He held her tightly, and as she laid her head on his shoulder, he stroked her hair. When she found the energy to caress his face, he pressed a kiss into her palm. That simple gesture seemed somehow the most intimate act of the whole night. It was tenderness distilled.

They showered together and dried each other with the hotel's big, fluffy towels, reveling in that intimacy. When she reluctantly drew away to head for her clothes, he followed and dragged them out of her hands.

"So that's how it is with you Ivy League business types. A red-hot quickie or three and it's off to the next poor, innocent musician?" He pulled her against his big, warm body. "The least you can do is stay and cuddle with me for a while."

She laughed but sensed an earnest desire beneath his teasing and let him walk her back to the bed. Climbing in with her, he pulled her against him and murmured that he could really get used to the feel of her in his arms.

Tears stung her eyes and she had to close them.

*This was every woman's fantasy...*

# 6

LIGHT WAS STREAMING in around the curtains when she woke the next morning and found herself facing a strange digital clock that nearly gave her heart failure. *Hotel room*, it said. And *ten o'clock*. She bolted out from under the covers and onto her feet, feeling as if she'd just gone twelve rounds with Brad Pitt, Ed Norton and the entire Fight Club.

The rasp of regular breaths nearby registered, and she whirled to find Nick sprawled across the other half of the king-size bed, snoring softly, sporting a serious case of bed head and beard shadow. Warmth washed over her.

She'd never seen anything quite so sexy in her entire life.

The heat rising through her was quickly dispelled by a draft of cool air that reminded her she was naked. A tingle of goosebumps spawned full-frontal flashbacks of last night's Nirvana. Whoa, baby.

Whoa.

Ohhh.

She backed away from the bed, unsettled by the thought that he might awaken and find her watching him with her heart in her eyes.

She hadn't expected to feel this way. Somewhere between the heart-stopping sex, the toe-curling intimacies and the mesmerizing music, the desire for *more* had taken hold of her. On the way to the Drake, she had convinced herself that a steamy night with the legendary Nick Stack would be the boost to her confidence and the workout her sex drive needed. And she'd have a heck of a memory to warm long winter nights.

But now she didn't want the memory, she wanted the man. She wanted to wake him up and have breakfast with him and spend the day with him and take him home to her apartment and show him her favorite parts of the city—

Oh, God. Her heart stumbled over the realization. She was thinking about somedays and tomorrows…a relationship.

*Get real, Samantha.*

By his own admission, he'd been in this same situation many times before. Nights like this were probably a dime a dozen for him. It was a sobering thought; one that called attention to a host of other less-than-comforting realities. He was a musician, a man with a very public past, a man whose every aspiration and experience was the opposite of hers. Men like him were *singles,* not long-play albums.

She had learned the hard way that one glorious night— even the best night of her life—did not a relationship make.

Tears sprang to her eyes.

*The best night of her life.*

She had to get out of there.

Tiptoeing into the parlor, retrieving garments from the floor along the way, she fumbled her way into them. No panties. She cringed. They were probably still wedged in the bedclothes somewhere. She was dying to use the bathroom, but decided to find one in the lobby rather than risk waking him. Biting her lip, she looked at the figure in the rumpled bed and then at the piano where they'd— The sight of the hotel robe in a heap behind the bench sent a painful surge of longing through her.

Leave. *Now.*

Outside in the hall, waiting for the elevator, she caught sight of herself in a mirror. Her hair had dried in five different directions, her lips were puffy and there was a pillow crease on her cheek. But it was her eyes that gave her away. They were soft and luminous, utterly sated. She groaned. She looked as if she'd spent the night in Olympic orgasm trials.

"Snap out of it." She pulled her jacket together and ran trembling fingers through her hair. "No purse, no keys. Not even cab fare. Where the hell was your head, Drexel?"

The aching fullness in her chest provided the answer.

It was following her heart.

She was out the Drake's front door, pulling up the collar of her thin suit jacket against the wind, when she realized she'd be walking into CrownCraft's offices in yesterday's clothes. Several blocks down the street in those aptly named "killer shoes," she had the idea to duck into Bloomingdale's and buy a new blouse and some underwear. She knew many of the saleswomen there and hoped they'd allow her to charge it to her account without her card.

But even the clerks she knew at Bloomie's needed to see a driver's license or photo ID. It occurred to her that she couldn't even get into the security-obsessed CrownCraft offices without her company ID. Her only option was to have her assistant locate her purse in her office and bring it to her.

By the time Renee arrived with her bag and the coat she hadn't thought clearly enough to ask for, Sam was so grateful, she greeted her with a huge hug. Renee studied her boss's rumpled appearance with a wry look but, to her credit, handed over the purse without a single question.

It was two o'clock before Sam arrived back at the offices, wearing a new blouse, underwear and sensible shoes…fortified by food and a venti latte. The sight of her coming down the hall with Renee brought Dale, Sarah and the rest of the team to their feet.

"So—" Dale followed her into her office while the others

clogged the doorway behind him "—how did it go, boss?"
When her jaw dropped, he clarified: "The shoot. Did we get
the photos or not?"

She tried not to look as sheepish as she felt.

"We got photos of *some* kind. Halcyon agreed to use our
lab here in the building and get them processed before going
back to New York. Dale, I want you to interface and give him
all the help he—" The phone rang.

"Our esteemed leader." Sarah pointed toward the ceiling,
indicating the executive floor and their VP of Marketing.
"He's been calling all day for a report."

Sam shooed everyone back to work, checked her hair in
the glass of a picture on the wall and headed for the elevator.

As she passed Dale's desk, she could have sworn she
heard him sing "'Yeah, bay-beee.'"

NICK SAT ON THE SOFA in his suite at the Drake, staring at
the phone, listening for the sixth time to Sam's voice-mail
recording. Where the hell was she? Why wouldn't she pick
up the phone?

But then, if she did answer, what would he say? Everything
that came to mind sounded like a cheesy song title. "I Feel
Good." "Baby Come Back." "One More Night." He had come
perilously close to singing one of them onto her voice mail.
Pride pulled him back before he made a compete fool of
himself.

Samantha. The syllables of her name rose and fell in his
mind like notes. With her, he had felt plugged into the
universe's main line, alive and full of creative juice. She
made him laugh, made him lust, and made him want to make
music about how she made him feel.

Then sometime during the night, she just picked up her
clothes and walked out, leaving him with a cold bed and a
morning-after full of memories. It had been a long time since

he cared if a woman took off while he was still sleeping, and longer still since any woman had made him feel such a wild mix of anticipation, arousal and *anxiety*.

He placed the phone back in its cradle, embarrassed by his eagerness. What made him think she'd want to see him again? Did he honestly believe that a few tunes and some sizzling sex would make her forget he was a has-been rocker without a record deal, a musician whose income and prospects depended on a fickle public...an ungrateful asshole whose behavior put others' jobs in jeopardy?

Two or three calls she might somehow "miss." But six? Heat crept up his neck, flooded his ears and finally ignited a burn in his face.

Who was he kidding? She had a fast-track career, and the looks and brains to make it to the top of her field. She'd taken a flyer with him, that was all. Scratched an itch. Satisfied a curiosity. She'd gotten what she wanted and was ready to move on to bigger, better things.

"Bigger?" he snarled. "Not freakin' likely. Not *better* either."

Still, when the phone rang some time later, he pounced on it.

"Ah, I caught you" came a man's voice. Nick's heart sank. "I was afraid you might already be at the airport." It took a moment to realize that those affable tones belonged to photographer Halcyon White.

"My flight doesn't leave until seven-thirty." Nick glanced at the suitcase waiting by the door.

"Is there any way you can take a later flight? I just finished the first prints. There's something you need to see before I hand these over."

"I don't have approval," he said, biting back the word *anymore*.

"I promised you some proofs and I think you should see

these before I present them to CrownCraft. They'll be ready in a couple of hours."

So, at eight o'clock that evening, while his agent was winging his way back to the west coast without him, Nick was being escorted through a darkened and empty CrownCraft building by a security guard. In the photo lab on the basement level, he was met by Halcyon White and an older guy with a graying ponytail, whom Halcyon introduced as Dale Emerson.

"At the end, I just snapped a few different angles and hit the jackpot," Halcyon said, leading him past a series of eight-by-tens drying on lines to a light box just outside the darkroom door. He handed Nick a lens and pointed to a specific frame on a strip of negatives. "Try this one."

Nick stared at the image, then looked up with a startled expression.

"Wait until you see it printed," Halcyon said, leading Nick back to the enlargements they had passed on the drying line. He unclipped one and handed it to Nick, who carried it to a brighter light and stared at it with such intensity that his hands began to shake.

"This one is special. It's the one I think CrownCraft should use," Halcyon said, watching him closely. "But it will have repercussions."

"Yeah. I get it." Nick's gaze was lightning-blue and crackling with energy when he looked up. "It's one hell of a photo." It had to be, to have changed his thinking, his mood and his plans in the blink of an eye. His smile grew until it became a wicked laugh. "By all means, *use it.*"

THE NEXT AFTERNOON, when Sam came back from lunch, she was met with an emphatic summons from Marketing's creative director. She found Halcyon White in the main conference room with designers and marketing execs crowded around like frenzied worker bees.

"There you are!" The photographer corralled her with an arm and ushered her through the others to the nearby light table.

"What's going on?" she asked as he handed her a magnifying lens.

"I've worked day and night getting these ready," he said, gesturing to the negatives. "This is good stuff, Samantha. *Really* good."

She glanced at head designer Dale, who looked ready to burst with excitement, then put the magnifier over the negatives Halcyon indicated. She blinked. There were *two* figures in the photo. She shot upright.

"I thought you said you were shooting around me."

"I did. Except in these last few shots." Halcyon nodded to Dale, who stepped aside to reveal a print enlargement of the photo she'd seen.

She and Nick were there in profile, staring into each other's eyes, backlit and revealed with amazing clarity. Even at a glance, the impression of longing, tension and *sex* was downright palpable. Their faces were all but glowing with desire. It was the very embodiment of awakening chemistry between a man and a woman, that precious instant when a whole universe of possibility unfurls before two people.

"What the hell is th-that?" She had to scramble for words.

"*That* is romance," Halcyon said with unmistakable pride.

"*That* is our CD cover," Dale added, grinning from ear to ear. "And our POS piece. And our mail-outs to Rewards Card participants." He regarded the poster-size enlargement with pride. "In short, that is the center of our whole marketing campaign."

The reality of it came crashing down on her.

"B-but that's *me*," she croaked. "I never agreed to be part of this."

"But you *are* a part of it." Halcyon trained his laserlike perception on her and gave her a knowing smile. "A big part."

"Look, Sam," Dale stepped in, lowering his voice. "Photos like these are rare in a photographer's career. This is a signature moment for Halcyon as well as us. When people get an eyeful of this poster, they'll stop to look, they'll sigh and they'll buy something that reminds them of love and romance—our products. This is the best POS inducement I've ever seen, and I've worked some pretty big accounts."

She looked around the conference room at the account managers and company execs staring speculatively at her. They were wondering just how far she'd gone with Nick after the shoot. And why wouldn't they? Her lust and longing were up there in living color for all to see.

Hers. She stared at the photo. And Nick's.

Heat surged through her skin. The moment captured in that photo, that intimate, naked flash of feeling, was a prelude to the most intimate and pleasurable night of her life. And unless she said something, it was going to be used to sell valentines and stuffed animals and cutesy slogan mugs. Nick's complaint about how they were "chopping up his best days to use as punchlines in valentines" came back to her with a vengeance. She understood with painful clarity, now, just how he felt.

Feeling the critical stares of her colleagues, she struggled to reframe the situation. It was business. It was just a photo. But another glance at that life-size depiction, and the kisses in the elevator, the whole night of sexual delight came back in a rush. Who was she kidding? This was as *personal* as it got.

After all of her hard work, it was excruciating to think that her biggest success might come from selling out—literally— her most private feelings. She felt as if she'd just taken a giant step backward for all womankind.

"There has to be— We don't want to—" She tried to think.

"There's our golden girl." A familiar voice announced the

arrival of the VP in charge of CrownCraft's Marketing Division. Ken Bentwhistle smiled broadly and straightened his Gucci tie. "Fabulous photos, Drexel. I've just been upstairs with the others massaging the numbers." *The others* meaning the company's flock of veeps and the CEO himself. She started to hyperventilate. "With a push, this campaign can rescue our sagging card and specialty sales. Christmas orders are down, but this gives us a focus for the new year. Brilliant stroke, Drexel, putting this Stack guy's music in our valentines."

Sam groaned. Silently.

Three days later, the letter from Legal arrived, requesting her signature on a release that would allow them to use her image in the campaign. "A formality," they said, as if it were a foregone conclusion that she'd sign. And as a smart marketing manager, why wouldn't she?

But it took two more calls from Legal before she sat down at her desk with the release form in one hand and a pen in the other. Nick had already signed a release in his original contract, which meant she was going to bear sole responsibility for plastering their faces all over America.

Her way of coping with the sly looks and questions aimed her way over the past few days had been to shake her head good-naturedly, as if she were in on the joke, then tamp her feelings deep inside and guard every word. But now she sat at her desk and stared at the legal verbiage through prisms of tears. What would he think when he saw the posters and CD?

Her gaze went to the phone. Should she call him and apologize? What would she say? That she was sorry for letting the company turn the best night of her life into fodder for a sales campaign? And how stupid would she feel if he laughed his butt off at the irony?

No. She finally allowed the memory to rise. He had enjoyed their time together as much as she had. But they were grown-ups. Consenting adults. He probably expected her to figure out that it was a one-time thing.

With an ache around her heart, she picked up her pen and signed the release.

# 7

TWO WEEKS INTO THE New Year, Sam came down from a meeting in the executive conference center with her face and pride on fire.

"This is your baby, Drexel." VP Ken Bentwhistle had waved a stack of messages at her in front of a room full of upper-level management. "Stack is trying to pull out of the appearances. If he doesn't show, we lose two sizable markets and all the publicity kick for this campaign. We've got too much invested to let that happen. I want you on this guy like white on rice. Babysit him, hogtie him—hell, kidnap him if you have to—but get him to those appearances!"

By the time Sam left the meeting, her face was scarlet and her stomach was in knots. She knew why he was refusing to come, and on one level she couldn't blame him; he'd finally seen the posters and CD cover. With barely a month to Valentine's Day, they were being hung and stacked and displayed in stores across the country. He couldn't miss them. He had to be furious with CrownCraft, their agreement and *her.*

She needed to call him and somehow get him back on board.

"Get me Stack's agent on the phone," she ordered Renee on the way to her office. Moments later, she was extracting apologies, concessions and Nick's personal cell number from Stanley Ripkin.

Closing her office door against prying ears, she punched

in the California area code and number. She finally reached him on the sixth call.

"Before you hang up, at least listen to what I have to say," she said the instant he answered, hoping to get her point in before the explosion.

"If this is supposed to be an obscene call, you've missed the—"

"It's Samantha Drexel at CrownCraft." There was a pause on the other end. *No immediate explosion.* She pressed her hand over her heart to muffle its wild beating. "I know you're probably furious, but you can't pull out of those appearances. It would be a disaster for you and us."

"Samantha, Samantha…oh, *Samantha.*" The way he said her name reminded her of the way he'd said it when they were… "The one the tabloids and paparazzi have been hammering me about."

She stopped dead in the middle of pacing from desk to door.

"Okay, I can explain—"

"This should be good," he said, voice compressed, reined. He was barely holding his temper.

"I *told* Halcyon that I didn't want to be in any of the shots. And he left me out of them, mostly. He caught a few of us in the same frame. And when he presented them to the company brass, the photo of us together was the one he insisted had to be used for the main part of the campaign." Silence on the other end. "He got all it's-one-of-the-best-shots-of-my-career and you have to admit, it has an impact."

"Impact," he said in clipped tones. "That's what you call it?"

"That's what the company brass called it. And they insisted on using it for the campaign. We've used others of you alone in print ads and press releases. But the poster is… I know it's awkward, but you can't use it as an excuse to back out of appearances. You have a contract, for pity's—"

"I'm not."

"You're not what?" She felt the tension squeezing her chest ease.

"Backing out because of the posters. Whatever else I am, I'm a pro at the publicity game, Samantha. I just happen to be a little busy."

Did he think she was a complete idiot?

"Doing what? What could possibly be more important than kissing babies and signing autographs at the biggest mall in Dallas this weekend?"

"Laying down tracks for an album."

That stopped her for a moment. She knew how important that was to him. A dozen questions clogged her throat, making it hard to speak. But she swallowed and managed to get past them.

"You have to be there. If you don't show, the company is going to sue your pants off."

Unexpectedly, he laughed. Her skin responded on its own with goosebumps. When his voice came again it was deep and husky and full of taunting sensuality.

"There are easier ways to get my pants off, babe."

Panicking, she hung up. She knew he'd said it just to provoke her. And his mention of tabloids and paparazzi... For the first time she considered the implications of the photo in *his* world. They were hounding him about his new flame? She tried to control an unholy tingle of excitement.

None of this was getting him to Dallas. When she had her temper and hormones under control, she called back.

"You have to go to Dallas, Nick."

"Yeah? Or what? You're going to come out here and get me?" There was male challenge in his voice. "Say, why don't you do that, babe? Just come on out to L.A. and *make* me go to Dallas."

And this time *he* hung up.

NICK CLOSED HIS PHONE and sat looking at it for a minute. He was taking one hell of a risk. He opened his cell again and called up a snapshot of the photo that had changed everything. Her face and his. The minute he'd seen it that night in Chicago, he'd known that every instinct he'd had about her was spot-on. She was something special, and together—Hell, together they were magic.

It was all right there in the photo for the world to see—wonder, longing, tenderness, desire, hope. And he wanted it. It shocked him just how much. With Sam Drexel there were no half measures. He wanted it all…the slow burn and the fast talk, the soulful surprise at the bottom of the box. He wanted to sink into her warm-honey eyes and feel that bone-deep sense of connection again. And again and again.

And if he played his cards right, she wouldn't know he was chasing her until she was his.

IT TOOK TWO INTERMINABLE days for her to get there. She walked into the control room of Studio A at Studio City Sound in L.A. wearing tall boots, one of those narrow skirts of hers and a sweater that hugged her curves like a second skin. He shot to his feet and ditched his headphones.

"What are you doing here?" he demanded, his throat tightening. The impact she had on him was all he'd remembered and more.

"Did you honestly think I'd let you sink both our careers?" She folded her arms and glared. "Look, I'm sorry about the poster and your tabloid troubles. But the flight to Dallas leaves in five hours and we're going to be on it."

A tall lanky guy in jeans and a Bob Marley T-shirt stuck his head in the door to say, "She pushed right past me, man. This the one?"

"Yeah. It's okay, Pete, don't worry about it," he said.

But the guy lingered in the doorway, raking Sam with an appreciative eye. "I see your problem. I'd tap *that,* for sure."

Sam looked as if she didn't know whether to be insulted or not.

"He saw the poster," Nick said, narrowing his eyes. "Somebody brought it in." Then he bolted past her to call after Pete, "Hey, is J.C. in? I want him to come and have a listen. I think I've got it down, but I need his ear."

Sam backed up, folding her arms, looking around uneasily.

"So you're coming with me?" she said, though it sounded more like a question than a statement. "I'd hate to have to knock you over the head and dump you in a trunk."

He took a little longer than was necessary to answer.

"Okay. But if the plane doesn't leave for five hours," he said, "I've got time to finish mixing this track." He pointed to a chair along the wall. "Park it."

And he donned the headphones again and went back to work at the boards. Not that he could concentrate with her sitting only a few feet away, six weeks' worth of tension and longing crackling between them.

SAM FELT TOTALLY OUT of her element as she took in the equipment, the records and framed photos on the walls, and the musicians hanging around the halls and control rooms. This was his world, his life, and it was a little unnerving to see him in it, working hard from the looks of things. His performances always seemed so cool and effortless, but here he wore a haven't-been-to-bed-for-two-days look. She felt herself warming dangerously. What was it he'd said he wanted to be—a good musician and *a good man?*

She watched him greet a short, stocky Hispanic guy wearing silk pants and a tropical print shirt, whom he introduced as J.C.

"She the one?" J.C. asked, extending one hand to her while shaking the other as if it had been burned. "Ayieeee, *muy caliente.*"

High school Spanish. *Muy* = very. *Caliente* = hot. Apparently he'd seen the poster, too.

For the next hour and a half Sam watched as Nick worked with J.C. on something, while musicians and technicians gravitated to the control room and sat around talking, seemingly waiting for something. They were a gregarious bunch who horsed around until Nick and J.C. removed their headphones and punched a button to release the sound through the speakers. Then every one of them grew serious and listened intently.

On came a low driving beat that set up a fabulous tension and made Sam ache to move. Bass and background were layered in and suddenly there was Nick's guitar, throbbing, crooning, seducing—it was so visceral she had to uncross and recross her legs and tuck her arms around herself to keep from bolting out of the chair. When the song ended, there were whoops, high fives and even some applause. Nick was obviously pleased. His eyes shone with what looked like pride.

"Now you see what was so important." His smile faded and his tone flattened, so even that it betrayed nothing but determination. Both went to her very core. "Now I'm ready to do Dallas."

Minutes later, they were in a cab and an hour and a half after that they were at the airport, having stopped by his modest apartment to pack a bag. They'd sat side by side in the taxi, stewing in tension all the way to the terminal. There they were consumed by the mechanics of security and catching the flight. And once on the plane, they were seated in totally separate areas—he in first class, she in coach.

At the Dallas end was another taxi ride and the hotel

check-in. He had a full suite with a piano; she had a double with a toilet that ran constantly. She had to pace for a while in her room before getting up the courage to confront him and establish ground rules for a working relationship that would get them through these appearances. Because, even hours later, she was feeling overwhelmed by her reaction to him, his music and the memories of their night together.

He answered the imposing door shirtless, wearing only a pair of jeans. He'd showered and shaved and she realized that his damp hair seemed slightly shorter, neater than in Chicago.

"I think we should talk," she said, and he waved her inside. As she stepped in, she was conscious of her body in relation to his. Stiff with tension, she crossed the parlor of the suite to check out the view, which was, of course, spectacular.

"In the interest of getting through these three appearances, I want to apologize for any discomfort you've suffered as a result of the company's use of that photo. And I want to assure you, we're taking steps to see that the publicity is focused strictly on your work. I suggest that if asked about the woman in the photo with you, you just say it was a spur-of-the-moment thing, a studio assistant asked to stand in…and let it go at that."

"A studio assistant." His face darkened. "So you're disavowing all connection to it?"

"Well, I was there in a professional capacity, after all. What difference does it make who I am?" She folded her arms, feeling strangely bereft as the words left her mouth. It didn't matter? She could have been any one of thousands of interchangeable females who had lusted after him? Everything in her rebelled at that idea.

"You know what really gets me about that whole *picture* thing?" he said, edging closer, looming over her. "The fact that you didn't bother to call me to warn me about it."

The heat radiating from him made her mouth go dry.

"I—I didn't know what to say. I mean…after—"

"After you slept with me?"

There it was. The plain truth. She took a step back.

"I thought you would probably misunderstand and be angry."

"Just what would I have 'misunderstood'? Why you slept with me? The fact that you walked out without a word the next morning? The way you avoided my phone calls the next day? That all seemed crystal clear."

"C-calls?" Her brain focused on the one word in that list with the potential to crack her defenses. He'd *called?* Yeah, right. But what if he had? "I didn't know. I didn't have my phone with me. And I wasn't in my office all day. I thought…"

Desperate to keep him from detecting the hope in her gaze and voice, she retreated. She backed into an overstuffed chair, which jarred her enough to engage her stalled brain.

"Look, it's common knowledge that you should never mix business and pleasure. When you do, sooner or later the business gets messy and the pleasure gets tainted." She was relieved to be able to produce such well-defined and irrefutable wisdom.

"Bullshit."

She looked up in surprise and felt her knees turn to rubber…which was the very reason she had avoided looking directly at him until now.

"I mix business and pleasure all the time, babe," he said. "I have to. In the music business, your life and the way you live it are all just part of the package. Hell, if I waited until I had privacy to do something, I'd still be waiting when I was packed off to a nursing home."

In two strides he crossed the space she had put between them and seized her shoulders.

"But since you've made it clear *you* don't mix business and pleasure, which was I?" he demanded. "Business or pleasure?"

The firmness of his touch and the electricity coming from him sprang the lock on a Pandora's box full of memories. Desire, embarrassment, defiance, longing, arousal; she was swamped by feelings.

"You—" her voice caught as she admitted "—were *special.*"

He gave a short, disdainful laugh.

"You can shovel it with the best of them, can't you? No wonder you're such an ace at marketing." He looked her up and down, making her wish that she'd worn a jacket over her snug sweater, that she could shove him back a few feet, and that her toes weren't curling in her boots. "What the hell are you doing here, Samantha?"

"Making sure this appearance goes off without a hitch."

"You sure about that?" He reeled her toward him…his movements deliberate, irresistible, a force of nature.

"Come on. What are you really doing, coming out to L.A. and hauling me all the way to Dallas? Are you chasing me?"

"Wh-what?" Her eyes widened as his narrowed. He slid his hands lower and pulled her tighter against him, watching her pupils widen.

"You came out to see me, didn't you?" His mouth quirked up on one side. "Yeah. Perfectly understandable. I'm probably the best you ever had. I rocked your world. I made you freakin' see stars and rainbows. Man up, Drexel, and admit it."

She gasped and pushed against his chest, but he wouldn't let her go.

"Come on, Samantha, tell the truth. No more bullshit."

"You can be *such* an asshole." She ground out the words, averting her eyes so he wouldn't see the humiliating moisture in them.

"I believe we already established that. But I can also be a pretty damned decent guy," he said, "if you give me half a chance."

Something in his tone brought her resistance to a standstill. As she softened, the force of his arms around her eased.

"That's what made me angry, Sam. After the time we spent and the love we made, you didn't give me credit for having honest emotions, for knowing the difference between a cheap thrill and the start of something that could be important. When you didn't…I thought you just saw me as some has-been rocker you could score bragging rights on."

The words resonated in her head, loaded with genuine feeling, a hint of hurt and a knee-melting glimpse of the real man inside. He, too, felt the anxiety of wondering if he would be good enough, if he would be accepted. It astonished her. And a moment later she was surprised by that astonishment. She really had thought of him as larger than life and immune to things like self-doubt.

"I did not see you like that," she said, bracing her hands against his chest. "You were never a has-been or a *score* to me."

"Business or pleasure, Sam?" The taunt was gone. This time, the question came from the heart. If there was ever a time for honesty, it was now.

"*Pleasure,* all right? It was just pure mind-boggling, world-rocking pleasure." Her gaze fell to his lips. "And it was confusing as hell."

A slow, sexy change came over his face, a private smile unlike any she'd seen on him before. Unashamedly tender, it was both the promise and fulfillment of understanding. It was a knowing that was both here-and-now and yet-to-come. It was a moment for sharing a decision that had been made weeks before. She closed her eyes and lifted her mouth.

Her knees buckled as the liquid lightning from his kiss

streaked through her. He filled her arms, her senses, her desires in ways she had never imagined anyone could. Just when she thought she couldn't hold all the joy erupting in her, he broke that luscious contact and backed away.

"Wha-at…what are you doing?" she managed to get out.

"Giving you some time to think, babe," he said, his chest rising and falling fast. Clearly this withdrawal was costing him, too. It had to be important. "The next time I ask you 'business or pleasure' and you answer, I don't want you to be confused. I want you to know exactly what you want."

He put an arm around her, led her to the door and brushed a kiss across her lips.

"Besides, if I start making love to you right now, we'll be up all night and I'll look and sound like hell at the autographing tomorrow."

She didn't know whether to applaud his clearheadedness or give him a swift kick for it. She turned on her heel and headed for the elevator, muttering.

"Now who's putting business ahead of pleasure?"

# 8

---

IT WAS A LONG, RESTLESS night for Sam. She heard every door slam from every room up and down the hall and the damned elevator seemed to run all night long. She had plenty of time to process what had happened between her and Nick that evening, and came to the conclusion that he was probably right. She was conflicted about what she wanted from him. He seemed to want her but something was holding him back, something big enough to make him to check his infamous libido at the door.

It was as if he was waiting for her to make the next move. Only she wasn't sure what move he expected.

She thought of the afternoon ahead and prayed that today's appearance went as she hoped. Because if it tanked, he might never speak to her again.

CROWNCRAFT HAD GONE all out to make Nick's three contracted appearances memorable, starting with a barrage of co-op radio and print advertising designed to reach romantically inclined thirtysomethings with disposable income. They had arranged for piped-in music—Nick's, of course—a stage and backdrop calculated to draw attention, and giveaways of dozens and dozens of roses and romantic Valentine's Day dinner packages. The Galleria had done promotion as well, billing this as "Valentine Preparedness Week," soliciting gifts and prizes from merchants.

It wasn't until they arrived in the mall's main court that she realized just how well the elements she had envisioned months ago had come together. Three twenty-foot-high banners hung behind a stage; two were valentine-red expanses reading "CrownCraft ROCKs ROMANCE" and the third, in the middle, bore the image of her face looking up into Nick's. The stage had baskets of red roses to be distributed to attendees later and a DJ from a sponsoring radio station was warming up the crowd with drawings and fun facts about Valentine's snafus.

The court was full and the railings of the walkways above were lined with onlookers. There were even handmade signs saying "We ❤ Nick" and "Stackman Rules" carried by young women pushing strollers.

It was difficult getting through the crowd to the stage, even escorted by mall security officers. Nick paused to survey the banners and staging, then bent toward Sam, seeming a little stunned.

"The place is packed," he said, shaking his head. "Is somebody giving away a car or something?"

"This is for *you*, Nick." She had to half shout in order to be heard. "They're your fans. Just like me." She met his eyes for a moment that seemed like an eternity. "They *love* you."

A dazed grin burst over his face and he wrapped an arm around her and hugged her hard against his side before pulling her through the crowd with him. When they reached the stage, he pointed to the front corner then bolted up the steps. She paused to flash her CrownCraft credentials and ask an event staffer if the guitar and amp she had ordered were ready. The staffer checked in with someone on his radio and then pointed to a couple of sizable amps and an electrified acoustic guitar propped against a stool at the rear of the stage.

The audience responded noisily to the DJ's introduction.

She headed for the front corner where Nick could see her, and was riveted by the sight of him opening his arms to greet the crowd. Tall, tautly muscled and dressed in black, he cut an unforgettable figure. When he spoke—his voice deep, earnest and sexy beyond belief—the women in the crowd giggled and groaned.

As the radio interview began, the attendees quieted, trying to hear. Nick was asked the usual questions: his favorite songs, inspirations for his albums, where he lived and if there was a special lady in his life.

There Nick paused and gestured to the banner behind him, giving a wicked laugh. "What do you think?"

"Well, who is she, this mystery woman?" the DJ asked, getting the crowd to applaud agreement.

"We're not ready to go public yet," Nick said. "But maybe soon."

There was audible disappointment, but then somebody from the back called out a question that the DJ picked up and repeated.

"Where've you been, Nick?"

Without a moment's hesitation, he responded.

"Living large and learnin' lessons, man. Learning lessons."

He smiled at how easy it was to admit. And just like that, something clicked and he knew—he was back in the groove.

The interview went on for a bit longer, then the DJ asked Nick for a favor—that he sing into one of CrownCraft's new recordable cards so he could give it to his own girlfriend for Valentine's Day. Nick obliged, giving his signature line, *"Yeah, bay-beee,"* all he had. The crowd loved it when it was played back. In fact, it was so successful that he did a couple more as giveaways for audience members, autographing them.

When the bomb came, Nick was having so much fun, he barely realized he'd been blindsided at first.

"So what are you going to sing for us, Nick?"

"Sing?" Nick chuckled at first, looking around. "This is an appearance, not a concert." That drew good-natured disappointment, but disappointment all the same.

"But that's what everybody came for. A song or two." The DJ turned to the crowd. "Right, people?"

Nick glanced at the faces of the crowd as they whistled and yelled.

"Without sound system or backup? I don't even have a guitar."

"*Au contraire,* Stackman," the DJ crowed, waving to the guitar and amps being brought forward by mall staffers. "We happen to have your favorite model right here."

Spotlights came out of nowhere and after a moment's consultation with the DJ, Nick shot a look at Sam, who nodded and smiled. After a few moments of preparation, he launched a rousing rendition of "Baby Tonight" that got the crowd going. The combination of the recorded version and his live voice made for a potent performance.

The DJ reappeared when it was over and asked, "How about some of this new stuff we've been hearing about?" He invited the crowd into the discussion. "What about it? Want to hear some new Nick Stack?"

Nick hadn't experienced stage fright since he was in third grade, but the past few years he'd spent his time writing and practicing, telling himself the music wasn't ready. He hadn't tested his new sound in anything bigger than a club. He felt himself tensing, and somehow thought of Sam.

"Okay, but I don't just sing this song—I have to sing it *to* somebody. Somebody special." His gaze focused like a heat-seeking missile on the corner of the stage where Sam stood. "And there she is."

He pulled her up the steps and seated her on the stool on the stage. She must have seen the doubt in his eyes, because she reached for his hand.

"You can do this, Nick." Her voice sank to that intimate, ear-tingling rasp that fired his blood. "Just do what you do. Play that song you played for me. Have fun and they'll respond the way I do."

He leaned down and kissed her, drawing oooohs from the crowd.

"Yeah," he said, setting up a sensual rumble in the mike. "She looks familiar, doesn't she?" And he glanced up at the backdrop and gave a low-down sexy laugh that evoked woo-hoos as the audience recognized her.

He began rapping a familiar beat with his hand on the body of his electrified acoustic guitar and graduated to that odd combination of tapping strings and drumming that produced such an amazingly full sound. It was "Baby Tonight"—his jazz version—and it showcased his voice so well that even Sam's jaw dropped.

The rising murmur from the crowd changed to astonished applause. Soon the crowd was singing along and gyrating to the music, the atmosphere becoming part concert, part "rolling party."

They liked it. His whole being relaxed. And when it came time for another song, he knew exactly which one he wanted to play.

THE MELODY SOUNDED familiar, but it took a minute for Sam to recognize the song he'd played for her at the hotel. She had to force herself to breathe as he spooled out a smooth set of lyrics.

"Eye meeting eye is how it begins…dancing, then holding, dreams start unfolding…touch to touch, and skin to skin…when do you start to let somebody in? When you feel a heart beat…next to yours… When you feel body heat… next to yours…."

She stiffened, gripping the edges of her seat, as she

realized he was indeed singing it to her. Her skin broke out in goosebumps the way it had that day in the studio. It was part rock, part jazz and all Nick.

"Body to body, you can't pretend…kissing, sighing, a sweet kind of 'dying'…we're daylight and night, we're prose and we're rhyme…the yin and the yang—between, beyond time. Come on and let me feel your heart beat…next to mine…come and share your body heat…baby…next to mine…"

By the time he got to the second break, her pulse was revved, her knees trembled from the strain of keeping them together and she felt herself sliding toward another sensual meltdown.

It wasn't just the music anymore. She looked up into his glowing face and silver eyes, and knew it was the man himself. For her, the music and the man were inseparable, and she wanted both with every fiber of her romantically susceptible being.

The song ended, and the crowd erupted in response. She rushed to throw her arms around him. He was sweaty and breathing hard, but he picked her up and gave her a lusty kiss in front of everybody.

The volleys of camera flashes and the glare of TV spotlights aimed at them seemed to go on forever. Nick insisted she stay nearby while he posed with fans and signed a hundred autographs. When they were finally able to call a halt and exit the stage, she was practically flash-blind. As Nick steered her down the steps, a video camera and reporter for *Entertainment Beat* appeared out of nowhere.

"Who's the girlfriend, Nick? How long have you been together?"

He slid his arms around her and pulled her back against him, giving them a sly, satisfied laugh for the camera.

"Not for publication, guys," he said genially. "And don't bother asking the event staff. They don't have a clue."

But they *did* have a clue, she wanted to protest. They knew exactly who she was—she had waved her CrownCraft ID at them earlier. By tomorrow she and Nick would be linked together in—television fanzines? The blogosphere? Internet gossip? Instead of being just an anonymous face on a poster, she'd be identified as his *amour du jour.*

She looked up at Nick as the reporter left and found him wearing a too-innocent smile. That kiss, this pose—he *wanted* them to get the right idea. As Nick took her hand and pulled her along, toward the Galleria's VIP room, she found herself marveling at the audacity of the man and at her own pleasure in it.

When they got into the car, she found herself quizzing him on what he liked and what he didn't about the venue and the way things were done. All the way back to the hotel, they talked about the possible impact of the publicity and the surprising turnout. Most important, he felt he'd truly reached the crowd. They had genuinely liked his new sound and wanted more.

"Don't think I didn't notice the fact that they had a stand-in for my guitar ready and had the sound system wired to go."

"I believe in being prepared." She smiled primly.

"Pushy broad, aren't you?" He grinned.

"I'm good at creating *opportunities.*" She sniffed.

"I couldn't have done it without you," he said, looking as if he were rocked to the bottom of his soul by that knowledge.

"Oh, you could if you found some other marketing genius who believes devoutly in your talent and possibilities," she said in mock seriousness. "But we're not a dime a dozen. You better hang on to me."

"Excellent advice." He laughed. Then he slipped his arms around her and pulled her onto his lap, running his hands over her and tugging her close for a kiss. The hum of expectation in her blood slowly became a roar.

They were going to have sex again, Sam thought, and her whole body reacted to the possibility. Her skin was suddenly aching for the hands-on sort of attention he excelled in providing. Images of fluffy duvets and piles of pillows…soft sheets…his hard body…the fireplace… unrolled like deep, sensual carpet in her mind. By the time they reached the hotel, she was squirming on the seat and getting rug burn from anticipation.

They kissed feverishly in the elevator, then again in the hall, but when they reached his suite, she was struck sober by the impact of what was happening between them. He sensed it and kissed her fingers one by one, slowing the pace.

"You realize," she said tartly, "I've seen you twice in my life and both times have involved sex."

"Bodes well," he said, "don't you think?"

When she reddened and looked a little conflicted he laughed.

"Afraid I'll think you're easy?" He pulled her into his arms. "Actually, it's not me you have to worry about in that regard. Someday, when our kids ask, you'll have to be the one to tell them we had sex two out of the first three nights we knew each other. And if I hadn't shown some restraint last night, it would have been *three* out of three."

"What?" She was astounded, then perversely thrilled. "*Kids?* Who said anything about kids?"

"I thought you were the one who liked to be prepared."

"Well, yes, but there's 'prepared' and there's 'cart before the horse.'"

"Then I guess this is the time to ask that question again." He searched her face. "Are you still confused?"

Her face, her eyes, her body all softened.

"Not in the least."

"You're the best, Samantha." He gave her his hottest, most breathtaking smolder. "In fact, you're the best I've ever had. You rock my world. You make me see freakin' stars and rainbows."

She laughed and a heartbeat later she was losing her breath, her thoughts, the rest of her heart to the man who'd taken out an option on it years before…with a song that rhymed "baby" with "lay me."

Damn. She threw both arms around his neck as he went for the zipper of her skirt. Maybe she *was* easy.

THE NEXT MORNING, Sam awoke nestled in the frothy white linens of Nick's VIP-size bed…to find it was past ten o'clock and Nick was already up. She headed for the shower and luxuriated in it for a decadent amount of time. When she got out, she was startled by Nick standing outside with a cup of coffee for her.

"Hurry up, babe. Our eggs are getting cold."

"How do you know I even like eggs?" she said, wearing a hotel robe and drying her hair with a towel as she padded out into the parlor.

Nick stood beside a table set with linen and a vase of beautiful red roses. Her eyes widened as she edged forward with halting steps to find a card with her name on it propped up beside one plate.

"For me?" She felt a tug of emotion in her chest as he nodded. She picked it up.

When she opened it, it was a valentine. A recordable valentine…one from her line. For the first time in her life she felt some of the joy and pleasure her work brought to others. With pride she opened it and heard Nick's voice sing clearly, "I want you to be my valentine—today and always. But we both have to be at a Valentine's Day concert in Chicago. So will you go out with me on February fifteenth?"

She looked up with tears in her eyes, then threw her arms around his neck and in her fullest, clearest Lauren Bacall voice, sang out huskily, *"Yeah, baybee!"*

\* \* \* \* \*

# THE TAKEDOWN
## Joanne Rock

For Betina and Lori, who made plotting this project so much fun. Thank you for bringing to life such wonderful characters!

# 1

"NO ONE SAID ANYTHING about a threesome."

The scantily clad female model glared at her two studly coworkers for the afternoon. The male models had just walked onto the set in photographer Tori Halsey's home studio, their hips swathed in leather loincloths that must serve as some art director's idea of caveman regalia. Apparently the loincloths weren't working for the suede bikini-wearing leading lady though. With a pout, she turned to Tori and tossed her fiery red curls.

"I am out of here!"

Thinking fast, Tori set aside her camera. She needed this one last shot before she could pack up for the day and forget about sex-drenched Valentine's Day photos for at least a few months. As a freelance cameraperson for CrownCraft, the greeting card company, Tori knew Valentine's Day notes were their industry's biggest sellers next to Christmas cards, so Cupid's holiday took up a large part of her work calendar.

Enter the caveman three-way.

Or exit, as it were. The redheaded model dodged lights and set props as she stormed toward her dressing room, leaving the two bare-chested studs behind.

"Angie, this shot will take us twenty minutes," Tori called after her, wishing her job didn't amount to sweet-talking temperamental talent so often. The Christmas shots were easier. She usually slated a skiing trip up north and snapped a few shots of snow-covered pine trees or cardinals alight-ing on window sills. Simple, easy stuff that didn't require social skills and afforded her time to pursue the more artistic work she enjoyed. But the romance-y Valentine's Day pieces still paid the bills that gave her independence from her close-knit farm family in New York State. "And I'll let you bill it as an hour, okay?"

"That's not the point!" Angie insisted, stomping her high heel for emphasis.

And how charming that the modern sexualized ideal of cave life involved suede bikinis and high heels.

"You're uncomfortable with the ménage à trois idea?" Tori peered back at the set where the two muscle-bound men had decided to do push-ups to pass the time. An old modeling trick that made the guys' veins stand out, the push-ups would serve the photos well. Assuming she ever got Angie back in the frame along with them.

"My grandmother shops in CrownCraft," she said under her breath, her blue eyes betraying the real reason for her ob-jection. There was genuine fear there.

Tori smiled. She could totally appreciate the way a family could judge you. Pigeonhole you as the "crazy artist." Decide that you weren't fit to take care of yourself with such a bohemian lifestyle. Heaven knew, Tori's two older siblings had sided with their parents a decade ago to decide Tori wasn't responsible enough to manage her own life. They'd added up her general impulsiveness, a passionate nature and one really bad decision and somehow came up with total in-competence on her part…. But she digressed.

Wasn't that why she'd moved to the opposite end of the country, so she didn't have to dwell on other peoples' opinions?

"Tell you what. We're shooting in black and white anyhow, so no one will recognize that distinctive hair of yours. And we can make this shot all about the guys' shoulders and your bod, so we'll just turn your head to the side, okay? Grandma will never know that it'll be you tucked between two hot guys."

Angie bit her lip and peered back over to the stud muffins, who'd swapped to one-armed push-ups by now.

"You're sure?" She didn't even try to rip her gaze away from the testosterone display.

"Absolutely." Tori didn't blame the girl for her hesitation, but if she were in Angie's shoes, Tori would have objected to the suede bikini with pumps rather more vigorously than being sandwiched between two guys. "I'll show you a test shot on the computer."

Tori barely had the words out before Angie fluffed her curls and sashayed her way back toward the men, eliciting appreciative looks long before she reached her mark on the floor where Tori wanted her to stand.

Another crisis averted.

It was all in a day's work at this time of year. With Valentine's Day only a week away, the traditional cards were already on the shelves, but the torment of taking sexy pictures continued now that CrownCraft had ventured into e-cards. They were really pushing into the youth market this year, and the highly stylized sex vignettes were somewhat of a Tori Halsey specialty.

Ha.

As Tori directed the he-men into their places on either side of Angie for the shot, she couldn't help but laugh at the idea of her bogus expertise. How did a woman with no sex life to speak of end up with this kind of professional reputation? It was ludicrous, really.

While her family would always view her love life through the lens of one risky mistake that time she'd hopped on a motorcycle with a guy she barely knew, she'd actually been very conservative ever since. Finding out the guy you'd taken off with for a weekend adventure in the Poconos had a criminal record would scare any woman straight. Of course, Tori hadn't been given any credit for cleaning up her act since then. And no one had ever known that the reason behind that mistake had been because she'd been only eighteen and heartsick over someone else....

Someone she needed to contact very soon if she was going to keep her end of that Valentine's Day manhunting pact with her girlfriends. She just hoped Luke Owens put in his semi-annual Florida appearance soon.

"Beau, could you move your hand a little lower on Angie's waist?" Tori called over the eighties dance music she'd cranked up to keep everyone relaxed and having fun. And maybe to keep her from thinking about her decision to seduce Luke after all these years. She hadn't made such a scary choice since taking up with that motorcycle dude. Seducing gorgeous, upstanding, wildly intelligent Luke would be risky for a whole different set of reasons. Mostly because Tori feared her old crush could come back to bite her in the butt if she wasn't careful. And speaking of butts... "I need your pinkie and ring finger straying south of the border."

While Tori set up all three of the models for the shot, she recalculated how long it had been since a man's fingers had trekked over *her* body the way Beau's did on Angie. Over a year. And even then, her last relationship had been all about companionship and comfort. The sex had been safe and enjoyably recreational, but hardly the kind of thing to inspire racy greeting cards. Yeah, she'd definitely overcorrected her life after her date for the Poconos had been arrested for leaving New York State while on parole.

Her phone beeped while she was taking the test shot, a welcome reprieve from a crappy memory, so she checked the text message while the photo loaded onto the computer for Angie's approval.

*"One week left till D-day, girls. Don't forget our agreement. This year, we tell Cupid to go blow and do the man-hunting ourselves. Smooches, Samantha."*

Gulp. Time was closing in. Tori flipped her phone closed and wondered if she'd been too passive in waiting for Luke to show up this year. What if he'd found a hot girlfriend back in New York, where he still lived for most of the year, where they'd both grown up? Luke had gone to high school with Tori's brother, Tim.

But in his life as a high-powered attorney, Luke had a major client based in Tampa, close to where Tori lived in St. Petersburg. He owned a vacation condo just down the canal from Tori's house on a small water inlet, and while he rented it out most of the year—including to Tori's family, who came down to check on her far too often—Luke put in an appearance at least twice each year to meet with his biggest client and snag some time fishing.

She'd been expecting him to show up ever since the end of January. What if he didn't come this time?

She didn't want to spend V-day alone, any more than her manhunting friends. But she hadn't left herself a lot of time, half hoping her love life would work itself out if she gave it time. Then she wouldn't need to hit on an old friend.

And old crush.

*How's that working for you, Tor?* She could almost hear her rule-following older sister's wise-ass voice in her ear. Tonya had taken charge of the family farm's accounting after getting her degree, marrying a man close to home and reaping praise from the whole Halsey clan for having a good head on her shoulders. Tori, on the other hand, had been the "flighty" one from the time she'd used her father's prize tomatoes as an all-natural dye to make homemade finger paints.

"The test shot is smoking, Tori." Angie's throaty voice called her back to the job and away from the impending manhunt. "I'm game."

Wasn't that what Tori had said to her friends a year ago? That she was game for turning dating into a competitive sport? Yet she'd procrastinated and ignored the whole thing until she was right back in the same situation—alone with no prospects on Valentine's Day. No man to kiss her senseless or wrap his hands possessively around her waist the way the male models touched Angie.

"Great." Tori forced a smile. "Then let's get back on the set and we'll finish this thing up in no time."

After which, she would find some of her old nerve and start hunting down Luke. She refused to be the only one of her friends without a man when February 14th rolled around this year. So even if it meant donning a suede bikini and pumps and draping herself across the seat of Luke's fishing boat, she would make sure he noticed her once and for all.

LUKE OWENS TIED UP his boat outside Tori's house, then juggled a Styrofoam take-out container in one hand and a bottle of wine in the other as he made his way toward her door. The teriyaki chicken and twelve-dollar vino hardly made for a gourmet meal to share with his best friend's sister, but since he'd been charged with checking up on the family hell-raiser once again, he figured it was good enough.

God knew, he hadn't wanted the job.

Peering back to double-check his twenty-five-foot knock-around speedboat where he'd left it tied beside Tori's small skiff, Luke spied only a handful of vessels on the water tonight. His condo sat just a little ways up the canal from Tori, but they were on opposite sides, so making the trip by water was faster. Besides, after a hellacious morning in court and a turbulent plane ride down from New York City, nothing else could have cleared his head like skimming through the waves while the dolphins came out to play.

Tori didn't fish or even "boat" in the traditional sense. She liked to take that little craft of hers out and sit in the middle of the water to commune with nature or something. Luke didn't really understand it, but he'd seen her out there at sunrise sometimes, snapping pictures of the waves and taking in the scenery. She'd told him once it was because she was a Pisces, which made about as much sense to him as the rest of her.

He dodged Daisy, Tori's black Lab, on his way up the walk and steeled himself for the unwise attraction that always came with seeing Tim's kid sister. They'd danced around the attraction more than once, but the timing had never been right and, bottom line, he'd never seen much they had in common. Tori had always been the wild child—the youngest and most adventurous of an otherwise grounded, conservative farming family in the small Hudson Valley town where they'd grown up.

She'd always been more interested in art and dreams than real life, opting to chase the sunlight with her camera at twilight than help her father bring in the last of his crops before the rain. As a hardworking kid in his dad's law office, Luke had far more in common with the rest of her clan than she did. He and Tori's brother, Tim, still got together to go fishing every couple of years and Tim usually stayed in Luke's condo when he came to Florida to check up on Tori.

But tonight, it was Luke's job. Tim couldn't make it down until later in the week. And apparently Tonya—the other Halsey sister—had gotten wind of some bet Tori had made to find a guy for Valentine's Day. The family was convinced she'd end up with another convict. Luke personally thought she had more sense than they gave her credit for.

Then again, with Tori, you could never be too careful. So

when he'd bought takeout for himself tonight, he bought some for her, too, figuring she needed to eat, as well.

"Tori?" He called through the screen door. He couldn't knock with his hands full.

Music pumped through the windows and the sound of laughter drifted on the warm breeze as afternoon faded toward evening. A guy's laughter. She had company?

Irritation fired along with completely irrational jealousy. Hadn't he conquered any misguided feelings for her? Yes, damn it. This wasn't about his old interest in a woman who was all wrong for him. This was about making sure she didn't invite an ax murderer to dinner because she thought he made an interesting photography subject. Or a misunderstood guitarist in some dopey alternative band.

Daisy wagged her tail and whimpered at Luke's feet, clearly hoping he'd open the door for her. And with an invitation like that, how could he resist? He couldn't put an end to Tori's Valentine's Day hook-up, but he could damn well remind her that her choices made her family worry about her.

Juggling the take-out containers, he pulled open the screen, stirring the wind chimes nearby, a homemade doorbell. The scent of jasmine wafted from the vine she'd trained around the door frame. Everything about her place announced her colorful, whirlwind personality.

"Tori?" he called again, just as he heard the distinct timbre of a low, masculine voice all over again.

A tinge of jealousy hit Luke as he set the wine and the chicken on the butcher-block island in the kitchen. Being the emissary of her brother gave Luke every right to barge in and find out what kind of guy was occupying Tori's living room right now. Quickening his step, he turned the corner out of the kitchen, only to find Tori sandwiched between two half-naked men while a sexpot chick in her skivvies watched on.

Gesturing wildly with her hands, Tori seemed to be explaining to the other woman how to—what? Touch the beefcake?

The pumping bass of the music disappeared as Luke's ears went deaf to all sensory input. Like a cinema slow-motion sequence, the scene before him unfolded with painstaking detail. The sexy grin Tori flashed the guy behind her knotted Luke's insides, while the sight of the caveman's hand on her waist made the edges of his vision burn. The soon-to-be dead man in front of her folded his arms in a transparent attempt to flex ludicrous muscles that didn't come from any kind of genuine labor. The goofball wasn't listening to a word she said, using all of his five brain cells to direct his limited attention toward the gap in her pin-striped, buttoned-down shirt where it revealed a white tank top edged in lace underneath.

Luke flexed his fingers and tightened them into a fist, anticipating the satisfaction he'd take in an uppercut to the jaw....

"Luke."

The sound of his name halted him in his progress across the room. Awareness of scent and sound returned, calling him back from giving in to Neanderthal impulses he'd never before experienced. He spied the camera in her hand and took in the wealth of lighting equipment. She wasn't engaged in kinky sex games with this crew. She'd simply been giving the female model some hints on positioning. And she'd probably been snapping pictures.

Seductive, sizzle-your-retina pictures.

"I brought dinner," he said finally, not taking his eyes off the dude drooling over Tori's cleavage, even after she extricated herself from her men friends.

"Really? I didn't even know you were in town." She stopped a few inches short of him. Was it his imagination or did she stand closer than usual? Her nearness commanded his attention, so he quit trying to stare down the jerk-off in the loincloth. Her eyes wandered over him with searching assessment. Thoroughness.

Nah. That had to be his imagination. He'd just gotten overheated seeing her with another guy. Some of that possessiveness must have spilled over into how he looked at her now.

"I got in an hour ago. I thought I'd bring over some dinner and see how you've been." He didn't have any intention of dumping off the food and leaving now. If Tori had any plans to rope in one of these dudes for her alleged Valentine's Day date, he'd bust up that idea by hanging out with her instead. These cavemen looked like they could be trouble. Luke had never liked the idea of Tori having her photography studio in her own home, with no one there to protect her but a black Lab that slobbered joyfully over anyone who crossed its path. "How soon will you be free?"

"We're almost done. You'll stay and join me?" She leaned down to pet Daisy and gently steered the dog out of the room at the same time. Her blouse gaped open again, and Luke felt like a traitor as his gaze landed right in the same lush valley that the caveman's had.

"Of course." He took Daisy's collar and waved Tori back to her photo shoot. "Finish up with the Stone Age thing and I'll find some plates."

Because there wasn't a chance in hell he was leaving until the gym rats had their clothes on and were out of Tori's house. It was an unwritten law in the big brother's best friend's handbook: half-naked horny men were not allowed near younger sisters. Period.

"Great." Straightening, she gave him another surreptitious once-over and grinned. "I'm *so* glad you're here."

She sauntered out of sight with an extra spring in her step and sway in her hips.

And while Luke knew that teriyaki chicken from Landry's Grill was one of Tori's favorite dishes, he couldn't help but think she seemed overly enthusiastic. Which was all well and good. He just hoped he'd be able to sit across the table from her without thinking about how at ease she looked shooting sexy photos. Somehow the sweet-natured farmer's daughter had grown up with a keen eye for sensuality that helped her capture eroticism through the camera lens.

Luke couldn't help but wonder if directing all those steamy scenes was enough for her or if she ever fantasized about recreating one of her own. Damn it. Of course she did. That was why she'd probably decided to nab some undeserving jerk for Valentine's Day.

His fists clenching all over again, Luke told himself there wasn't a chance in hell she'd make a bad choice with him around. In fact, seeing her again made him realize he could rearrange his schedule to stick around town for another week or two, just to make sure she didn't end up in the Poconos on a whim.

And that decision didn't have a damn thing to do with the sudden excitement he felt at the sight of her open blouse.

## 2

FATE WASN'T LETTING HER make any excuses this Valentine's Day, apparently. All that time she'd been stressing about where she'd find Luke and if he'd come to Florida in February and then—*zap*. He ended up in her living room at the exact moment she'd been contemplating a wild affair with him.

Tori spied on Luke through the crack in her bedroom door. He was setting the table with her plastic picnic dishes while their dinner reheated on the stove. She'd dashed into the bedroom after the models left, supposedly to change her clothes. But mostly she wanted a chance to think through her strategy before she acted on her impulse to seduce the quiet, outrageously successful attorney pouring wine into juice glasses she didn't remember she owned.

He was definitely scrumptious with his tall, lanky frame and easy athleticism. She'd always thought he had a great face. That chiseled jaw took her breath away. She'd had a crush on him eons ago, but he'd always been so serious— focused first on his studies and, later, on his fast-paced career. She, on the other hand, had taken a while to find a profitable outlet for her quirky blend of artistic skills. She'd always known she wasn't his type. Although there'd been that one night… It had been at her college graduation, when she'd had a smidgeon too much to drink. She'd had the distinct impression he'd hit on her.

Of course, he'd never reiterated the interest when she'd been *sober,* leading her to believe he'd imbibed a bit too much that night also. He knew as well as she did they didn't add up on paper. But maybe her attraction to him hadn't always been one-sided.

Still, after college, she'd been ready to leave her suffocating family behind and set out for parts unknown. The next time she'd seen Luke, at her family's Christmas party that year, he'd had his arm wrapped around a lady geophysicist who studied rocks in Brazil or something.

She was pleased to see Luke was all alone tonight.

"Dinner's ready," Luke called, glancing up toward her bedroom door and almost catching her spying.

She jumped back, flustered. Was she crazy to even think about coming on to Luke when they'd have to see each other at family parties for the rest of their lives? But then, why else would Fate send him here, today of all days?

She didn't consider herself superstitious, but she also wasn't foolish enough to ignore a news flash from the universe. She might as well go for it and put the man out of her head once and for all.

"Coming," she called, breathless at the thought of flirting with him. "It smells delicious."

He set the wine bottle on the table near his plate and dished up their dinner while she fought a sudden bout of nerves. He must have dropped by his condo and changed before dropping in, because he now wore faded cargo shorts and a shirt with a detailed artistic rendering of a fish she didn't recognize.

"Have a seat." He held out her chair for her with the same cosmopolitan deftness that had always set him apart from other guys she knew back when they were younger. Now, the intimacy of slipping into the seat while he tucked her close to the table made her breath catch.

He smelled fantastic. His aftershave teased her senses for a moment, and then he was gone, sitting beside her at the round pub table she used for meals.

"You must have left work early today," she observed, her body sending all kinds of happy signals that told her it was really on board with this plan.

Too bad she didn't have a clue how she was going to bag this big game…yet.

"I did. But even when I don't have an early flight, I've been trying to leave on time on Fridays so I can have some sort of social life." He speared a bite of chicken. "A guy can't work all the time."

Her pasta stuck in her throat.

"Are you seeing someone?" Visions of him with some elegant socialite daughter of a gazillionaire flashed through her head as jealously pinched.

"Not lately." He took a sip of his wine and his hand brushed hers as he replaced the glass on the table. "But the thought's definitely occurred to me. More wine?"

She realized she'd guzzled the entire contents of her glass at the thought of Luke being taken. Clearly, the idea of hitting on him had grown on her more than she'd admitted to herself. She wouldn't write off this encounter as another case of bad timing. Not after he'd shown up right before Valentine's Day, at a time when she'd been thinking about him so much.

"I'd better not." She moved her glass to the other side of her placemat so she wouldn't pour any more without thinking. The last thing she needed was a repeat of that night they'd both indulged a little too freely and said things they hadn't meant. If anything interesting were to happen this night, she wanted to be sure they were both very well aware of it.

"What about you? Got a guy in your life?" His warm chocolate gaze landed on her and lingered, making her feel the effects of the wine. Or maybe, it was just his effect on her. Whatever it was, she felt warm and tingly inside.

Until she realized why he asked.

"My brother put you up to this visit, didn't he?" Now that she thought about it, Luke asked her a similar question every year. Indignation rose.

Daisy barked, possibly catching the vibe. The dark Lab peered up at Luke expectantly.

"I'll take that defensiveness as a...yes?"

She noticed he'd dodged her question neatly. Leave it to a lawyer.

"No." She needed to make that clear, even if Luke wasn't asking out of any personal interest. With any luck, he'd have a personal interest sooner or later.

Too bad she still had no clue how to go about shifting this relationship from friends into something more. It'd been a long time since she'd hit on a guy. She hadn't trusted her judgment for a long time after her romance with the ex-con.

"No interest in the cavemen?" he prodded, polishing off his bread and cutting another slice. "Because the one with the mermaid tattoo was definitely checking you out."

"Hardly. He was barely twenty-five years old. Guys that age check out every female over eighteen in a three-mile radius. I think it's a biological fact."

Which brought home to her how much more discerning a man like Luke would be. He was a few years older than her at thirty-two. He knew what he liked and wouldn't get roped into some torrid affair with her just because of rampant hormones. She needed to go about this with skill. Finesse.

"Is that right?" He tipped back in his chair and she realized he'd finished eating while she'd barely touched her food. "Sounds like you've got it all figured out."

"Growing up on a farm put all the he-man posturing into perspective." She'd been raised alongside goats, sheep and dairy cows in the ever-changing menagerie her father called a farm. He'd gone green and "off the grid" long before either were cool. "Males of a certain age seek to mate all the time. Females decide who they want for partners and when they're in the mood. If they don't send out the signals, the males move on."

Luke said nothing, his expression inscrutable. Prompting her babble reflex.

"What I don't know, however, is if the females can ever successfully initiate the mating dance," she continued. She couldn't think of any examples of that in nature. Females were either willing or they weren't. They didn't hunt down a guy so they wouldn't be alone on February the fourteenth. "I think humans are unique in this. Sex for us is often purely recreational."

And wow. Hadn't she talked herself into a corner? She braved a glance at Luke while she reached blindly for her wineglass and found it empty.

"I'll drink to that." Luke grinned as he picked up the bottle and refilled her glass. "To recreational sex."

Her heart fluttered in her chest. Was this her opening? A moment of flirtation where she could suggest there be something more between them.

But then he clinked his glass against hers, not even waiting for her to lift it, and downed the rest of his wine. He tipped back in his chair with a self-satisfied smile and folded his hands behind his head. The exchange had been friendly and not flirtatious in the least. Hell, her brother would have drank to recreational hanky-panky, too. Men liked the concept. That didn't mean they were ready to engage in the act with someone they'd pretty well considered a kid sister their whole adult life.

So, fueled by wine and determination, Tori made her proposal anyhow.

"Maybe we should have some."

ALL FOUR LEGS OF Luke's chair hit the floor with a jarring thud.

"What?"

Luke recalled that his brain didn't always operate well around Tori, especially when the conversation ran to topics like sex. So he had to have misunderstood her comment. No way could she want what he thought she wanted. She must be asking for him to pass the bread. Or pour her more wine.

Anything but engage in a recreational hook-up.

"Sex," she clarified, her eyebrows raised meaningfully. "We're both unattached—"

"No." He had to put the kibosh on this fast, before it turned any more awkward. He'd known she was impulsive but— Holy hell. His blood simmered at the thought of what she suggested. "You're right about the whole recreational sex thing and I agree it's fun in theory. But, Tori, we've known each other forever—"

"All the more reason to consider a pairing that won't be a total disaster—"

"And you're Tim's sister."

He hadn't meant to interrupt her and she appeared fairly miffed that he'd done so. Or maybe she was miffed that he'd nixed the idea so fast. Either way, her arms were folded tight, her shoulders tense and straight as she glared at him across the table.

Still, he couldn't believe she'd suggested it. He'd come over here to steer her away from making a bad decision and— Crap. Maybe *he* was her next bad decision. Talk about being between a rock and a very damn hard place.

"You've barely given it any consideration," she pointed out.

Ah, that was rich.

If she only knew how much consideration he'd given it at different points in their lives. But his occasional fantasies about Tori had always been just that—delectable mental diversions. He couldn't afford to mess up his friendship with her whole family because she had some wild idea to…

His mouth went dry just thinking about it.

"Can I ask what brought all this on?" he asked, edging past the sawdust in his throat. She'd never looked at him in a romantic way before. He damn well would have noticed if she had. "You're not on the rebound. Why the sudden rush to…"

He couldn't even say the words.

"Get laid?" she supplied, a mischievous gleam in her mossy green eyes.

A cool breeze off the water drifted through the screen door and almost blew out the flame on a tall taper jammed in an empty wine bottle near the stove. He'd seen that look on her face before.

She'd cast that same wicked grin his way right before she stole the keys to her father's ATV, long before she had the license to drive it. And just as she'd roared off on the back of some guy's Harley. Her look said she was ready to make trouble.

And there was no way he was going to let her talk him into joining her in mayhem. One of them could damn well end up hurt.

"I can explain why there's a sudden rush," she assured him, switching gears from wild-eyed troublemaker to— oddly—a rational businesswoman in a flash. Standing, she waved for him to follow her as she turned away from the table. "But you need to see it to believe it."

She swished past him in the lightweight linen skirt she'd put on for dinner, her bare feet silent on the hardwood floor as she headed for her living room. Luke wanted to lift his gaze from the subtle swing of her hips as she moved, but apparently her outrageous proposal was messing with his head. Because he watched her like he'd never seen her before. A small ankle bracelet made of tiny bells jingled as she moved, and the rolled-up sleeves of her white cotton dress shirt exposed a tattoo on her wrist. He vaguely recalled hearing that she'd had the Japanese ideograph for destiny inked on there some time in college. No doubt she'd had it done moments after that devil-may-care gleam lit her eyes.

"Have a seat." She pointed toward a love seat near the area she used for her studio.

No sooner had he made himself comfortable than she'd plunked down beside him, snagging her laptop off the coffee table on the way.

"We're surfing the Web?" He couldn't imagine what was on her computer that could possibly explain her haste to hook up.

He *could* imagine how sitting this close to her would wreak havoc on his self-control, though, especially given the topic at hand. The scent of her shampoo already teased his nose, the clean coconut fragrance taking him back to the day he'd brought her to a shooting range for her twenty-third birthday. He'd idiotically thought he'd show her how to use a gun in case she ever needed to protect herself. He'd forgotten that a farmer's daughter would know her way around firearms. But there'd been those moments before she'd actually fired, when she let him show her how to level the weapon and his chin had grazed the top of her head….

The memory was blasted out of his brain by the image Tori brought up on her computer. It was a photo of a man and woman in the rain, under the shelter of an apple tree. The dude was stretched out on the ground—no shirt and a pair of jeans coming undone—while the chick crawled over him on her hands and knees. The woman's rain-soaked dress hugged her curves, as tantalizing as the whole rest of the scene.

Any hope Luke had of keeping a lid on his libido was vanishing. What the hell was she showing him this for?

"You see?" Tori tapped the computer screen with the backs of her fingernails, sending a ripple of distortion through the image. "*This* is what I do all day long."

Fire scorched his veins at the thought of her in a soaking-wet dress. His brain slowed its functioning.

"Straddle half-naked men?"

"Photograph sexy encounters."

Yes, that made more sense. Still, the heat in his blood didn't ease. Awareness of the woman next to him made his hands itch to touch her. It would be so easy to wrap an arm around her and press her back against the sofa cushions.

But oh, man, he was beginning to see her point about being around hot images all the time.

"A lot of people would think your job sounds fun—"

The words dried up on his tongue as she clicked through a series of eight or ten other photographs in a blur of changing erotic scenes. A black and white of a man and a woman in the backseat of a taxicab, the man's hand palming a fishnet-clad thigh as the woman's trench coat slid open to his touch. A man and a woman in an elevator, where the woman was tugging the guy's dress shirt off while she placed a kiss in the middle of his chest. A close-up of a man's hand dragging a strawberry over a woman's hip bone.

And on and on it went....

"Fun?" she asked, lowering her voice to a seductive whisper as she continued flashing the stream of photos. "Would you call what you're feeling right now 'fun,' Luke?"

Words escaped him. What he felt was the need to shove aside her computer and re-create every decadent, pulse-thrumming scene. With her. Right here. Right now.

"This is a low blow," he finally ground out between clenched teeth.

"I agree completely." She closed the laptop with a snap and set it back on the rolling work cart she used to store equipment for her photo shoots. "It is miserably unfair that I've created a niche for myself in a market that is getting hotter and hotter every year. You saw what I was photographing today."

She made a sweeping gesture toward the set, where she'd shot her cavepeople earlier.

"The model was freaked out that I wanted to shoot a *threesome*," she continued, shaking her head. "And who can blame her? What will they be asking me to photograph a year from now or the year after that? I'm so overheated now that I can't imagine facing my next assignment without some…outlet. Last Valentine's Day, I was so out of sorts, I vowed I wouldn't let another February 14th go by without— you know. Making an effort to be with someone."

The rant came to a surprisingly quiet conclusion. Her gaze turned to his and lingered as her mouth pulled into a soft pout.

His heart slammed against his ribs at the invitation, his temperature already spiked from the photo montage. His teenage fantasy woman was inviting him into her bed. And even though he knew it wasn't wise, temptation howled through him like a hurricane wind.

But how would he cope with the aftermath—of knowing he'd been just another one of her wild impulses?

"I—" He didn't know what to say. The only words that came to mind were emphatic yeses, avowals of her sex appeal or commands to remove her clothes. With an effort, he searched out the only answer he could give. "We need to think about this before we do something we might regret later."

Harder words had never been spoken.

She inched closer, tendrils of long blond hair falling

forward over her shoulders, framing her breasts. Eve and the apple couldn't have been more enticing. Luke knew he was seconds away from losing this battle.

"I don't understand." she said.

Standing suddenly, he put his body in motion before he acted on his every red-blooded impulse. Heat stoked his insides and crawled all over his skin. His fingers clenched at his sides with the need to sink into her flesh and mold her body to his.

"I'll call you."

And without another word, Luke headed for the door.

## 3

"AND THEN HE JUST *LEFT?*"

Tori closed her eyes at her friend's incredulous tone as they sat on her back patio at sunset the next day for drinks. She'd been friends with Barbara Bradley for as long as she'd been a photographer and Barbara had been a fledgling entrepreneur with a small modeling agency to service the Tampa-St. Petersburg area.

"He said he'd call me," Tori added weakly, realizing how pathetic her non-date with Luke sounded now that she'd spilled her guts to her friend.

She didn't usually share details of her love life with anyone—although some of that had to do with a very sketchy track record—but the lemon bellinis Barb had whipped up were strong. Tori'd found herself midway through her disastrous dinner tale before she second-guessed the wisdom of sharing something that made her sound like a total loser.

"Well, something's obviously holding him back," Barb diagnosed from over the rim of her frosted martini glass, her aviator shades propped up on her sleek, dark chignon. "If it's not another woman, my guess is he's freaked about the fact that you're his best bud's younger sister. That crosses a line for some of those noble types."

"It's not like I'm sixteen or something." Tori hadn't been able to just write off the embarrassing encounter as a gamble that hadn't panned out. Her feathers had been majorly ruffled. Luke's rejection felt personal.

"You kinda like this guy, doncha?" Barbara didn't let her Long Island accent run free unless she was around people she was comfortable with, but she distorted her vowels all over the place as she teased Tori.

"Of course." Tori tried not to make a big deal of the suggestion as the scent of a neighbor's seafood on the grill made her stomach growl. "He's been a family friend for ages so I like him well enough."

"You care about this more than you would if he were just a friend," Barbara announced, standing suddenly and slicing some more lemon for their drinks. "Trust me, I can tell these things. Although I wish you would fall for whichever one of your neighbors is grilling tonight. Doesn't that smell fantastic?"

Tori couldn't comment since she was still trying to process Barbara's insistence that Tori harbored deeper feelings for Luke. What if it was more than just an old crush?

"Luke *is* hot," she confessed, remembering what he'd looked like without a shirt. He'd visited the local swimming pool almost daily when he'd returned home every summer during college.

Then again, he looked damn fine even with a shirt.

"Honey, I need food to absorb all the alcohol I'm consuming, so let's discuss the merits of your lawyer friend while we're raiding your kitchen." Barbara pulled Tori to her feet and led the way into the house, where she proceeded to open the fridge, the pantry and most of the cabinets.

"Here." Tori snagged a package of frozen tofu burgers. "I'll throw these on the grill. But you have to help me come up with a manhunting strategy."

Barb plucked the sleeve of burgers from her fingers and tossed it back in the icebox.

"I don't know what tofu comes from and I won't eat it."

Then she proceeded to grab cheese, crackers and a knife and waved at Tori to sit, apparently taking charge of the food. "And since when do you need to resort to strong-arm tactics to get a man to notice you?"

"Since I sent one running for the hills last night."

"You wouldn't rather focus your attention on a man who *won't* run from you?" Barbara wielded the knife with the smooth efficiency of a sous-chef, slicing and dicing her way through the cheddar and moving on to a sliver of leftover Gruyère.

"I didn't choose a guy based on how quick he'll sleep with me." Tori straightened in her chair, shaking off the bellini buzz, trying to assert a little dignity. "I want Luke because he's a great person."

"Who also happens to be hot." Barbara nodded slowly as she divvied up the cheese between two plates. "Got it."

"So what do I do now?" Nervous excitement pinged through her. She tapped the wind chime made of tiny jingle bells near her kitchen window, the trilling sound an echo of her restlessness. "Bring *him* dinner? Ask him out?"

Barbara put the knife down with a thunk. "You just did that, remember? And it didn't exactly yield results. Geez. This situation calls for stealth, not a full-frontal assault."

"Stealth?" Tori considered her ability to be forthright one of her better qualities. Her practical nature and her willingness to tout her skills without modesty had propelled her career forward for years.

"That's part of the hunt." Barbara dragged her plate over to the seat near Tori's at the kitchen island. "Let's face it, if your quarry knows you're on the prowl, they're going to take cover. What you need is a guerilla attack so you can get close to this guy before he knows what hit him."

Tori munched a cracker and debated the approach. "That's not too underhanded?"

Barbara poked her in the shoulder in rebuke. "Do you want him to notice you as a woman or not?"

Hmm… Another Valentine's Day alone at the bar with her friends? Or a night of torrid passion with the sexiest male she knew?

Her heartbeat answered the question. Her pulse spiked at the thought of Luke's hands all over her. Luke's mouth on hers. Luke in her bed.

And oh, man, she needed to fan herself.

"I want to do this." Hadn't she paid the price for her mistake long enough? She'd tried to stifle her impulsiveness and focus on work, instinctively behaving like a Halsey even though she'd once sworn she'd die before she acted like the rest of her family.

She *would* reclaim her life outside of work. And this time she'd *live* the fantasy instead of photographing the fantasy for the rest of the world to indulge in.

"Great. I've got the perfect plan." Barbara pulled her sunglasses off her head and set them on the island. "Now I just need you to show me those pictures you were looking at with him before he ran out…."

TWO DAYS LATER, Luke prowled his temporary office at his law firm's satellite branch in downtown Tampa, his cell phone in hand. He came here whenever he was in town to touch base with their company's sole long-distance partner and a handful of junior attorneys. The branch wasn't big, but it was growing and they'd recently bought a penthouse-level suite at an office building downtown. Luke had met with his biggest client based nearby this morning. Now, though, he couldn't focus on anything else until he talked to Tori.

He'd called her twice since he walked out of her place Friday night, but she hadn't answered and hadn't called him back.

As he listened to her voice-mail announcement for the third time, he disconnected without leaving a message and wondered what the hell had happened between them. He'd had time to think about her suggestive proposal. Actually, he'd thought of little else since then.

And even though her offer had made him want her more than ever, he still didn't see how she could have made the suggestion so lightly. Did she make it a habit to proposition men?

He didn't believe that for a second, but damn. Her family would flip if they knew she was really taking this Valentine's Day deadline seriously. And she was obviously looking for the kind of torrid affair her family worried about, ever since her Poconos disaster. At least he wasn't a con man, unlike some guys she'd considered worth her time in the past. Who might she turn to next if Luke rejected her proposal?

He didn't want to tell Tim about this—no way could he tell Tim about this—but her brother had texted him twice over the weekend to find out how Tori was doing. What could Luke say? Yeah, she's fine, only her erotic photos have inspired her to troll for a man to help her act out her favorite scenes?

Or had that last part been a creative twist on her proposition? She had him in knots.

Pacing over to the window overlooking the street, he watched an afternoon rainstorm kick into high gear, spattering the glass and falling in sheets on the pavement below.

If he ever got a hold of her, he planned to find out how she thought a man and woman could go back to being just friends after—

His thoughts disintegrated as a car pulled into a parking space outside his building and deposited a woman in a trench coat. Even from five floors up, Luke noticed the hint of dark stocking on her legs as she emerged from the car. Seeing the rain-drenched woman in that distinctive garment reminded him of the sexy photos Tori had shown him. There'd been one of a drenched couple sharing a kiss in a cab.

And damn it. No wonder Tori'd had a tough time focusing on her work when the job required sensual fantasizing for creative inspiration. Pounding his fist on the glass in frustration, he turned on his heel and left the office. He needed some air.

A short elevator ride later, he was in the lobby of his office building, bolting for the door…and nearly bolting right past the woman in the trench coat, who studied the directory of offices.

Now, close up, more than her costume looked familiar.

"Tori?"

He stopped dead in his tracks at the sight of her long blond hair undone and wet with rain. Her curls had turned dark and kinky, falling in dripping spirals over the shoulder of her lightweight, belted coat.

"Hi, Luke," she said brightly, then turned back to the directory.

As if they were the most casual of friends, ones who hadn't recently contemplated sleeping together. Frustration fired through him.

"Can I help you?" he offered with exaggerated politeness.

"Actually, I've decided to incorporate my small business for tax purposes. Are there any attorneys you'd recommend in your firm?" She tapped the glass covering the list of professionals in the building. "I remembered you had this minibranch down here, so I thought I'd work with someone from your extended company."

She shifted from one foot to the other, drawing his eye down to her legs in dark silk hose. Just like in that damn picture on her computer. Did she run around town testing out the wardrobe choices from her shoots?

"Yes. Me." He reached for her as a handful of administrative types returned to the building after the lunch hour. "Come to my office."

She retreated a step, out of his grasp.

"I don't think that's wise, given what's transpired between us, do you?" She hugged a small leather folder to her chest, a case that no doubt contained the paperwork for incorporating her business.

"Nothing happened," he reminded her, steeling himself against the rush of male interest in what she was wearing beneath her coat.

The woman in the photo she'd taken had flashed garters in the scene. And didn't that provide a visual he could do without in plain view of the whole building? A tic started in one eye like a mini heartbeat.

"Not yet." She winked. "But why mix business with pleasure, just in case? Besides, I like the sound of Suzanna Maryweather. I'm sure she'll take good care of me."

Clutching her leather binder, she turned in the direction of the glass-walled elevator overlooking the lobby.

The tic in his eye started pounding like a jackhammer.

"We need to talk." He seized her by the elbow and turned her toward the set of private elevators, needing to speak to her alone before his retinas fried from the sensual wanderings of an overactive imagination.

"If you insist," she demurred, glancing at the silver watch on her wrist as he pressed the button for his floor. "But I've got another appointment after this."

"And who the hell would you be going to see dressed like this?" He'd waited until the elevator door closed behind them, sealing them inside alone.

"Like what?" She peered down at her wet raincoat and dark stockings. "I put on grown-up shoes and everything. No flip-flops. Even Tim would approve."

Did she honestly not know what he was talking about?

"You're wearing the same clothes as that woman in the photo—" He halted the words as the elevator opened again.

Thankfully, there was no one else standing between them and the door to his temporary office, so he hustled her past the small reception area and into the corner digs that had been vacated by a junior partner for his use.

"What woman in what photo?" Tori asked, digging in her heels just outside the door with someone else's name in brass plated letters.

Her voice was loud enough to attract the attention of a few research assistants and clerks in the middle offices. Unwilling to figure out how to introduce her right now when all his gray matter was devoted to what she had on under her coat, Luke tugged her inside his office and shut the door firmly behind him.

Then he locked it.

"The woman in the photograph you showed me on your computer the other night," he supplied, allowing his gaze to finally linger over her the way he wanted to.

A small rivulet of water followed the delicate curve of her cheek until she swiped it away. The lapel of her jacket gapped a little, revealing an enticing shadow where a hint of clothing should be.

What if the stockings were the only thing she was wearing under there?

"Don't tell me those pictures got to you after all." She set the leather binder down on a nearby chair. "I thought you were immune to my dilemma."

She walked to the same window where he'd first watched her emerge from a cab earlier. Staring down at the traffic, she focused her attention on the view while he couldn't rip his away from her. The belt of her jacket nipped her waist to practically nothing.

"Nobody said that." The rush of possessiveness that came over him was fierce. Primal.

Her hands went to the belt and untied it. Her back was still toward him and his heart stopped. His breath ceased.

Would she really do this here? Now?

Desire surged. He was already moving in her direction, already committing to the affair he probably shouldn't have.

As she turned to face him, however, she wasn't even close to naked.

A wrap dress draped her curves respectably, covering her in pale gray silk. He'd let his imagination run away from him and now here he was, inches from her. Ready to back her onto the desk and take her, even though she hadn't been thinking along the same lines as him at all.

"Luke?" She looked up at him uncertainly, her eyes tracking his as he tried to figure out his next move.

The scent of her rain-washed skin made the decision for him.

"I've been thinking about that proposition we discussed," he managed to say, completely incapable of holding back now.

He skimmed a knuckle along her cheek. A fire roared to life inside him. He had to touch her. Besides, if he didn't scratch this particular itch for her, who else might she find in his place? The thought of having anyone other than him touch her was unacceptable.

"And?" Her tongue swiped along her top lip, a soft, surreptitious invitation.

"And I think we owe it to ourselves to find out if there's any chemistry between us."

Then he slanted his mouth over hers, answering that question for her. By the time he was through with this kiss, there wouldn't be a doubt in her mind their chemistry was off the charts.

# 4

VICTORY WAS SWEET.

Toe-curling, mind-swirling and heart-racingly sweet. Tori swayed on her feet and clutched Luke's shoulder to steady herself under the spell of his kiss.

Heat streaked through her limbs, jacking up her temperature and steaming her rain-soaked trench coat. She hadn't expected such immediate results from Barbara's crazy plan to re-create the sexy photos that had sent Luke bolting from the house the other night. But apparently, still waters ran deep. A wellspring of hot passion lurked behind his teasing smile and lawyerly shrewdness. Maybe Luke Owens had an impulsive streak of his own. He kissed her like a man who knew exactly what she wanted and how to give it to her. Like a man far more skilled at this game than she was.

His mouth played over hers, tugging her lip between his teeth before he licked the same spot. He cupped her jaw, holding her still and tilting her where he wanted her. The base of his hand rested on the throbbing pulse in her neck while his fingers spanned her cheek. His thumb urged her mouth open to deepen the kiss.

A wave of pure want weakened her knees and her hips fell forward to meet his in a carnal invitation she hadn't fully intended. But now that she was there, his thigh parting hers as he backed her against the window, she couldn't imagine pulling away. His chest pressed hers, the hard expanse of muscle giving no quarter. She reached to open the lapels of her coat wider, wanting to feel more of him.

Just then, he ended the kiss.

She had a vague mental image of herself, dazed and confused, as she groped around for his shoulders again, blindly seeking more. Wrenching her eyes open, she found him watching her through narrowed lids, his breathing as hard and fast as her own.

Not sure what happened, she slipped her hands around his waist, close to the place where their bodies still touched. He seemed to snap out of the daze then, and eased away from her gently, prying her fingers from his belt to hold them between his palms.

"Was there any chemistry for you?" he asked politely, shades of his usual reserve coming through the steaming-hot new side of him she'd discovered in the past five minutes.

How could a man speak to her with such ruthless control when she'd nearly stripped off her clothes to get close to him a mere moment ago? And holy Trident's staff, had he been looking at her like this before and she'd never seen the intense attraction until now?

The possibility knocked her even further off center. Only now, she didn't have the benefit of Luke holding her up.

"Did you know that was there this whole time?" She couldn't even think how long they'd known each other.

"Is that a yes?" he pressed, pursuing the answer to his question like the attorney he was.

"I'm breathing like I'm hyperventilating and my lips are so tingly it's like I stuck my finger into an electric socket." She planted her hands on her hips, irritated with his calm rationality in the face of this monster revelation. "You tell me if that's a yes."

He gave a clipped nod.

"Then you can appreciate why we shouldn't play with fire."

She blinked, sure she missed a whole sequence in the conversation.

"Excuse me?"

"The chemistry between us is another reason we shouldn't mess around with some hare-brained short-term affair." His dark hair grazed his left eye, just above the scar that made him look like he was contemplating seduction. "You can't play around with that kind of heat. Someone will get burned in the end."

"I'm sorry." She tipped her head sideways and pounded on her temple. "I must have rainwater in my ears. Did you just say that we shouldn't sleep together *because* we're attracted to one another? I must have misheard you since that defies every biological law of nature."

"Tori, I want you. Badly." The simple truth of his words was still evident in his eyes now that she knew what to look for. God, she'd been blind not to have seen it before. "But I'm not going to settle for a night or two with you to scratch some itch you're feeling just because it's Valentine's Day."

If her skin hadn't still hummed with the raw power of his touch, she might have given him hell for that comment. As it stood, she was simply determined to make him see the light. Drawing in a steadying breath, she wondered what Barbara would have suggested. They hadn't brainstormed past the point of re-creating the scenes from Tori's shoots.

"Most people would say that attraction is an excellent reason to explore an affair." Swallowing her pride and the warm remnant of the sensual buzz he'd inspired, Tori gathered the belt of her coat and tied it. "But if you're not interested, I'll just go see the lawyer about my paperwork and get out of your way."

She picked up her leather binder and headed for the door, hoping Luke would act on whatever chemistry he apparently felt and take her on the desk. Against the wall. Anywhere would be fine.

But he remained where he was.

"Friends respect each other too much to have meaningless affairs," he called after her. Confusing her.

"Friends also don't tease each other with sex," she reminded him.

"I'm not the one wearing the trench coat."

Ah, damn.

Beaten in this round, Tori retreated until she could figure out what to do next. Because there wasn't a chance she'd walk away from chemistry like this without trying to make Luke see things her way. Today only proved she'd been right to pursue him. But if he thought she'd serve up her heart on a silver platter for him first, or give up her man hunt before she knew if there could be anything more than sex between them, he had another think coming.

"WHO WAS THAT AND DOES she have a sister?"

Luke had still been trying to screw his head on straight when the law firm's only resident senior partner barged into Luke's short-term office. Dan Walker had been with the firm for as long as Luke. They'd started at the New York branch together and had been friends ever since they'd been stuck doing a few overnight stints in the firm's law library during those early years.

"I don't know what you're talking about." Luke picked up his phone and pressed some random numbers while rattling around the papers on his desk. "I'm really swamped."

Dan walked to the desk and depressed the button to disconnect the call Luke hadn't really been making anyhow.

"We reviewed case loads this morning, remember? You're not busy." He pulled the receiver out of Luke's hand and returned it to the cradle. "Now fess up. Who's the hot chick?"

"No one you need to know." Luke knew how Dan dated. The guy had a new girlfriend every other month. There wasn't a chance in hell he'd let him near Tori.

"You're seeing her?" Heedless of the high-end suit he sported, Dan dropped into a chair on the other side of the desk and propped his feet on a low table. "Because if you're not, it's unfair to keep her away from the rest of us who actually live in the same town as her and could show her a good time."

Memories of the kiss he'd just planted on Tori's mouth returned with a vengeance. Judging by the way she'd sunk into his arms and wrapped herself around him, he'd say she'd been having a damn good time with him. The moment had been so hot and so sweetly gratifying, he'd been hard-pressed to find the will to let her go.

"I'm not seeing her." He damn well wouldn't until she got over the insane idea to just sleep together for the fun of it.

Too late, he realized Dan wasn't the best confidant for that bit of honesty.

"Then you'd better pass along her digits before anyone else takes a crack at her." Dan yanked a sticky note off a pad and slapped it on top of the papers in front of Luke. "Women like that don't stay single for long."

Possessiveness fisted in Luke's gut.

"Maybe when hell freezes over." He tossed the notepaper in the trash. "She wouldn't be interested."

"Why don't you let her decide?"

Luke shot him a warning glare that—thankfully—shut him up. For all of two seconds anyway.

"You like her." Dan sat up straighter. "Don't leave me hanging here, dude. Who is she?"

He shook his head, unwilling to discuss Tori.

"She's someone I need to look out for, okay?" He stood, irritated with Dan and keyed-up from seeing Tori. He was about to usher his colleague out the door when a woman cleared her voice at the entrance.

Tori stood there, still clutching that leather binder.

"Sorry to interrupt, but the attorney you recommended has left for the day—"

"I can help you." Dan was by her side in a flash. "My office is right this way."

Luke saw the guy's tactics for the shove in the back that they were. Still, he had the feeling if he didn't get Tori out of here right now, Dan would ask her out by the day's end.

And what if Tori decided his buddy would make a good candidate for her Valentine's Day hook-up?

"Does it look like hell has frozen over to you?" Luke asked, picking up his keys off his desk and tapping the switch to shut off his desk lamp.

"What?" Tori appeared confused, looking from Luke to Dan and back again.

Dan, on the other hand, didn't appear all that surprised. He gave an easy grin, one that had won over lady law clerks and random happy-hour females alike back when they used to hit the bars after work.

"We'll talk about this on the way home," Luke clarified, ignoring his friend as he ushered Tori past Dan and out of the office. "I'll give you a ride and we'll get the paperwork settled in the car."

Shutting the door behind him with a slam, Luke hit the button for the elevator, more than ready to have Tori to himself.

Dan's interest helped Luke realize that if he was serious about protecting this woman, he didn't trust anyone else around her before Valentine's Day. Anyone but *him,* that is. Luke couldn't deny that his old attraction for her had flared up with a vengeance.

And while they weren't right together for the long-term, maybe she'd be better off with him in the here and now. At least until he could convince her that this was no way to start a real relationship. That she deserved better than a temporary lover.

Damn, he was just rationalizing something he flat-out wanted like his next breath.

"I don't understand." she protested, peering over his shoulder…

…looking toward the womanizing showboat who would scoop her up in ten seconds flat if Luke didn't get her out of here fast.

He wrapped an arm around her waist and pulled her close as the elevator doors opened.

"I'm taking you home."

# 5

"THIS ISN'T FAIR."

Tori folded her arms and shot Luke a chilly glare, incensed at having her advances refused earlier. Then, the moment another man showed interest in her, Luke suddenly couldn't wait to spend time with her? She would never have guessed he could be such a hypocrite.

"What?" Luke eased her binder out from under her arm. "That I take care of filing the papers on your business, or that I offered you a ride home?"

"That you accuse me of wanting a meaningless affair." And that was just for starters. "That you won't entertain any thought of being with me, but you won't let me spend ten minutes in the company of a man who might easily be persuaded—"

"Is that what you really want?" He jammed the emergency button on the elevator, halting the lift between floors.

A fire alarm sounded somewhere in the building.

"What are you doing?"

Had he lost his mind?

"Do you honestly want your fifteen minutes of fame with a guy like that, who takes every woman he meets to bed?" His eyes narrowed, his focus no longer on the binder he'd taken from her. He wasn't happy with her, but she couldn't help some small thrill of satisfaction that he was damn well paying attention now. "Didn't the incident with the ex-convict teach you to at least date casually before escalating things?"

"Do you know how long ago that happened?" She couldn't even believe he'd bring that up after a decade. "And, yes, I've learned a lot about dating since then. Mostly, I suck at it. But I can't ignore my judgment when it comes to men forever because of one misstep. And frankly, I'm not interested in having you play guardian to me when you're not planning to explore the kind of chemistry that takes your knees out from under you."

She was still reeling from that kiss and the knowledge that there'd been some kind of mutual attraction between them all along. An attraction Luke had ignored.

Since Luke glared at her in silence, she took the liberty of reaching to hit the emergency button again. The lift whirred back to life, shuttling them down to the parking garage level.

The motion seemed to snap Luke out of his stupor. His expression shifted to something even more inscrutable.

"Has it occurred to you that I want to play guardian because I care about you?" He took a step toward her, closing the distance between them to a few negligible inches.

The proximity touched off a skip in her heartbeat as her senses went back on high alert. She said nothing and he stepped closer still, forcing her back against the rear wall of the small cabin just as the doors opened on the street level.

Why did he want to play white knight? How could he think she needed saving, just like her family? Didn't he understand her well enough to know that the last thing she wanted was someone trying to stifle her sense of adventure when she'd finally found the courage to take a few chances again?

"Tell me, Tori," he pressed, never missing a beat. "Would you even be interested in me this week if it wasn't for this Valentine's Day mania?"

She steeled herself against the raw appeal of his remembered kiss. If she didn't extricate herself from him now, she could easily fall under the spell of this man. And she wasn't ready for the kind of relationship he alluded to. Not when she'd worked so hard to blaze her own trail in life.

Right now, she needed to leave and regroup. Rethink what she wanted since a "simple" affair wasn't going to happen with this man. He was too calculated. Too deliberate. He'd never do anything without good reason, and maybe for him, red-hot chemistry just wasn't enough of a justification.

So, edging past him out into the lobby, she put a safer distance between them, even though her tingling skin protested the move.

"I get stuck with Valentine's Day mania all year, thanks to my career. So I consider myself a trooper for thumbing my nose at Cupid for years. And just so we understand each other, I'm *not* in the market for a protector. On the contrary, I'm looking for a man who's ready to walk on the wild side and not look back." She took a deep breath, knowing her blood wouldn't cool for a few hours at least. "If you're ever ready to be that man, you know where I live."

LUKE TIPPED HIS FACE into the spray kicked up by his boat as he returned from a fishing trip later that week. He'd hoped the quiet time on the water would help him figure out what to do as far as Tori was concerned but he was still as frustrated and keyed-up as he'd been two days ago when she'd stepped into her car outside his law firm and taken off without a backward glance.

He could have stopped her. He'd even planned on taking her home with him after his talk with Dan made Luke realize he didn't want anyone touching her but him. But something she'd said had rattled around his head—something about not trusting her judgment. Luke had regretted bringing her past back up, but maybe he'd needed to hear for himself that Tori had changed. She wasn't the wild child of the family anymore. Luke had guessed as much, based on the success of her business and the fact that she'd carved out a nice life for herself far away from her family's influence. But hearing about the whole Valentine's Day manhunt had thrown him for a loop. Made him think maybe she still didn't take enough time to evaluate dating prospects.

But maybe he just hadn't wanted to think about her with anyone else.

Now, he slowed the engine as he steered his way from the bay into the channel between the houses on the water. He hadn't caught many fish and what he'd taken, he'd already cleaned and stored. The boat still needed to be hosed down tonight, but Luke had showered in the craft's tiny bathroom before the trip back, knowing he'd pass Tori's house on the way.

Knowing he would stop.

She wanted a walk on the wild side? He planned to take her there as soon as possible. And while she'd been ticked off at him two days ago, he had chemistry on his side. She'd even admitted as much.

Twilight fell, though the sun hadn't fully set, streaking the sky pink while the homes along the water began to brighten up. Pathway lights flicked on with daily timers, the whole neighborhood in almost perfect sync.

Except, of course, for Tori's place.

He could see the little bungalow as he rounded a pie-shaped lot that bulged out into the channel. Tori's home was a vintage 1930s structure, a Florida original just like its owner. The farmer's daughter hadn't molded her home into the upper-middle-class suburban style, preferring a few torches near the water and a line of paper bag lanterns lining the walkway from the water. In fact, he spotted her now, lighting those very lanterns with a long stick, a modern-day fairy in a batik skirt and bare feet.

He cut the engine, but she never even glanced up from the lanterns as she moved along the stone path. A shadowy canopy of bougainvillea blooms blew in the breeze from an arbor spanning half of her yard. With no noise from his boat to drown out the sounds around him, he could hear some folksy, bluesy singer wailing out a tune from her yard. She must have a speaker propped in her kitchen window again, a trick he knew she used when she wanted to have drinks or dinner on her patio.

"Tori." He didn't mean to call her. The name slipped from his lips as he found himself surrounded by so many things that made her the unique person she was. The container garden that bloomed year-round with one thing or another. An orange tree that had never been touched with pesticides.

Wind chimes. Night-blooming jasmine.

She straightened as he tied off the boat, her stiff posture evident even in the last purple light of dusk.

"Hi." She nodded as she blew out the flame on the twig she'd used to light the lanterns.

Up until this past week, she would have waved him inside like she always did when he stopped by during his semiannual visits. Smiling. Comfortable.

As much as he missed the warmth of her sunny smile, he was grateful tonight that "comfortable" was no longer a facet of their relationship. Now that he'd made up his mind to take her up on her steamy proposition, he could hardly restrain himself.

"I brought you some snapper." He didn't grab the cooler though. Filling her freezer was mostly an excuse to see her.

"Thank you." She reached for the scarf tied around her hair and loosened the knot, unleashing the mass of blond waves to fall around her shoulders while the silk floated to the ground.

The gesture was more careless than purposely seductive, and just like that, Luke recognized her most powerful sensual weapon. Sure, he'd felt a thrill at the sight of all the sexy photos she'd snapped that first night at her place. And seeing her in that trench coat, re-creating one of those scenes, had aroused him even more. But nothing attracted him quite as much as Tori in her natural element. Vibrant. Unaffected. Coaxing beauty from everything around her.

"Is that all you wanted?" She walked closer, an ankle bracelet jingling with each step until she stopped a few inches away from him.

He had to clench his fists to keep from reaching out to her.

"No." The scent of night jasmine and her shampoo washed over him, drawing him deep into an attraction unlike anything he'd ever felt before. "I wanted to apologize for the way I acted that day at the office."

Her nod was small, almost imperceptible, unless you knew her well.

"I'm sorry I suggested you'd have a meaningless affair with anyone." His eyes wandered over her shoulders bared by the skinny straps of a purple tank top. "I know you better than that."

"I probably shouldn't have been so blunt in my original proposal anyhow," she admitted, shifting her stance so that the ankle bracelet chimed again. "I'm sure it sounds crazy to you that I could be so influenced by the Valentine hoopla, but honestly, my work is so full of hearts and flowers and sexual innuendo that I'd have to be a robot to be immune to it."

His mouth went dry at the thought of her arranging all those provocative photo shoots. Lighting half-naked bodies for the most titillating effect. Dreaming up the most seductive scenes to capture the imagination. He wondered how long he would have lasted without an outlet for the heat her job stirred.

"It would get under anyone's skin," he agreed, more

certain than ever he had to act now on this attraction. She wouldn't stay single forever.

He was damn lucky he hadn't already missed his chance.

"You're not just saying that to make me feel better?" She raised a suspicious brow, but he heard the teasing note in her voice.

Just like old times.

But he wasn't retreating to safe territory yet. Not when there was still a chance he could use an affair as a starting point. A way to get close to her.

"No." He reached for her hand and twined his fingers through hers, his thumb idly circling the place where the destiny tattoo lay, right on the throbbing of her pulse. "And if I wanted to make you feel better, I wouldn't use words to accomplish the deed."

TORI WOULD NOT LET herself misread the cues.

So if Luke wanted to think she was horribly slow-witted, that was okay. She refused to make the first move with him again when he'd been very clear about how he'd felt regarding a physical relationship with her.

For this reason, she did not fly into his arms like scrap iron to a magnet. Instead, she held herself utterly still while her brain struggled to understand his words.

Her body hot and bothered, her mind foggy with desire and confusion, she remained mute. Unyielding. It was only the urgent beat of her heart she could not control, and it reverberated through her so loudly she knew he must recognize the storm inside her.

But just when she thought she could stand no more, he wound his arm around her waist and dragged her close. His mouth covered hers and she had all the clarification she needed. The manhunt was over and they were both going to enjoy the spoils.

Restraint fell away like grain to the thresher. She released his hand to wrap her arms around his neck, pressing her breasts to the hard expanse of his chest. Excitement hummed and tingled. A million different sexy images flashed through her mind, recalling all the times and all the ways she'd wished she could try out the seductive vignettes she dreamed up for her photo sessions. With him.

His mind clearly made up where she was concerned, he backed her up the stone pathway until her rump met the resistance of a tree trunk. His body surrounded hers, his flesh simmering with heat as she moved her trembling, wandering hands over him. Any thought of what they once were to each other burned away as she touched him. She could never see this man as a mere friend. His kiss was so consuming, so frankly sexual, she felt like his lover already.

Or maybe that was just what she wanted to be.

The night breeze ruffled her skirt, lifting the sheer fabric until he helped it along, gathering her hem in his hands. She shivered despite the mild evening, anticipation coursing through her darkly as her mind's eye pictured what they must look like. Her—suspended against the porch post, melting for want of him. Him—keeping her captive with a touch that set fire to her senses.

For a long moment, he didn't put his hands on her at all. He simply held her skirt high, letting the breeze have its way with her while his tongue plundered her mouth. She gripped his shoulders tight to steady herself, her fingers fisting in the cotton of his clean T-shirt.

Then, breaking the kiss, he lifted her hair to speak into her ear.

"Unless you want me to undress you right here, you'd better come inside with me."

Blinking away some of the sensual haze, she calculated the steps to her bedroom. Even the kitchen table was too far.

"The hammock." She pointed toward the far corner of the porch where a length of canvas tied between two posts was hidden from the water by the bedsheet she'd hung out to dry earlier in the day. The white cotton fluttered gently, the eyelet edging snagged on a honeysuckle hedge.

"Perfect," he murmured, looking into her eyes.

Wrapping her arms around him, she held tight as he lifted her. He carried her to the oversize swing and deposited her in the middle of the slack fabric.

For a moment, he watched her in the moonlight, his gaze undressing her. His hunger spurring hers. She broke the moment by slipping her hand into the waistband of her skirt and shoving it down. Off.

She sat before him in a purple thong and purple tank top, her breath coming so fast she felt like she'd run ten miles. Her skin hummed with anticipation. The bedsheet tickled her thigh as it blew restlessly in the breeze.

She thought maybe he would join her on the hammock, but his eyes never left her as he shrugged his way out of his shirt. She'd seen him without it a few times. But the sight had never made her pulse spike the way it did now. Her hands trembled with the need to touch him.

She reached for him, her fingers skimming the flat, planked muscles of his abdomen. Tanned and smooth except for the dark sprinkling of hair down the center, the muscles clenched at her touch. He started to sink to her level, but she stopped him, her hands working the clasp of the belt buckle.

He hissed a breath between his teeth as her fingernails grazed the flesh she exposed. Deliberately unhurried, she eased down the zipper of his cargo shorts, freeing the straining length of his erection. As he stepped out of the shorts, she felt him through his boxers, the heat of his heavy flesh sending an answering jolt of fire through her.

When he sank to his knees this time, she didn't protest. He anchored the swing with his body, preventing it from rocking forward as he pulled her into his arms. Kisses rained over her neck and shoulders, his hands sliding beneath her tank top and bra to free hooks and ease the garments over her head. They landed on the honeysuckle bush, she realized hazily. Right now, she was most concerned with the way his touch ignited her skin as he claimed every square inch of it.

"It's only been a few days since I got here, but I feel like I've waited so damn long," Luke whispered, his breath a steamy caress over the damp skin where he'd kissed the swell of her breast.

The crests tightened and ached. All of the sexy photographs she'd ever taken combined couldn't stir half the heat this man's kiss could. Her back arched toward him.

"I'm not letting you wait another second." Her soft curves grazed the stubble of his jaw, spurring him to action.

He pulled one taut peak into his mouth, rolling the tip between his teeth with exquisite care before drawing deeply on the swollen tip. She cried out, her thighs restless and her panties moist with want.

She spread her legs, inviting the hard bulk of his body between her thighs. He growled deep in his throat at the contact, the vibration sending a pleasurable thrill through her.

He reached between them to play his fingers over her womanly heat. The thin layer of cotton separating her from his touch was a negligible barrier and with one swift yank, he tore the skinny straps of the thong.

A soft moan filled the air, a lush, needy sound she realized came from her. She'd never been so overwrought, so ready for sex.

He broke away from her for a moment and she reached blindly for him, her nails scratching his shoulders to bring him back. In a moment, she realized he must have undressed and found a condom, because the thick base of his cock pressed against her, already sheathed.

The contact sent a sweet, convulsive shudder through her. Not a full-blown "O," but a precursor that told her tonight was going to eclipse every sexual experience she'd ever had.

"You like that, Tor?" The raw, masculine edge in his voice raked her senses. Arrogance and hunger were a compelling combination.

She squeezed her thighs tighter against his waist.

"I'd like more," she demanded, ready to remind him he wasn't the only one who could provide pleasure.

In an instant, he was on his feet, poised above her. She kissed, licked and nipped his chest while he positioned her where he wanted, spreading her thighs with warm, strong hands. Until at last, the tip of his erection nudged the slick center of her. Pushing, gliding, filling.

Pleasure converged from every direction, congregating deep inside her. Her nails sank into his hips while her ankles locked behind him. Keeping him close.

The sound of his ragged breathing filled her ears as he bent over her. Holding her. The hammock swung beneath her just a little, molding to her the way she molded to him. Pleasure coiled all over again until it exploded in a starburst behind her eyes.

She shouted with the bliss of it. Waves of pleasure dragged her down like an undertow, keeping her captive to the lush, exotic spasms that shuddered through her. She didn't know how long that sensual spell lasted, but by the time she could breathe normally again, Luke had lain down on the hammock beside her. His big, gorgeous body followed the lines of hers, his chest to her spine. The fronts of his thighs cradling the backs of hers.

Never had she known such completeness. Her emotions swelled as they lay there, the breeze cooling their fevered skin even as the reality of what she'd just experienced began to sink in. Luke had told her all along he wasn't interested in some temporary affair. And sure enough, lovemaking had touched something much, much deeper inside her.

She could hardly contain the sweet secret her Valentine's Day manhunt had revealed. She just needed to figure how to tell him he'd been right all along. Their relationship deserved more than an affair.

But oddly, while it had been easy enough to chase Luke using Barbara's sexy strategy for manhunting, Tori wasn't as confident she could convince him one night together had made her realize she wanted more. Shyness tied her tongue until she decided simply to enjoy the moment. Nestling contentedly in the safety of his arms, Tori let the happiness of her discovery comfort her as surely as Luke's strong muscles enveloped the rest of her. She just hoped one night together hadn't changed Luke's mind about what he wanted out of this, the way it had changed hers.

As the moments ticked by without a word, without him offering any sense that their encounter had been as monumental and life-changing for him as it had been for her, doubt crept in along with the tide. She'd been so focused on being with him, so caught up in the sensual spell of fulfilling a longtime fantasy, she hadn't thought about ironing out what to expect from one another. Had he come here tonight on her terms?

Or his?

Because as much as she wanted to explore the heat between them—and the sweet new tenderness that followed—she wouldn't let him stick around if he wasn't interested following this attraction wherever it led.

# 6

SHORTLY BEFORE DAWN, Luke forced himself from the hammock. His time with Tori had exceeded his imagination—and he'd worked up some amazing dreams about her over the years.

But he refused to make her feel cornered. She'd been very clear about wanting to keep things simple and straightforward between them, so he wouldn't be the one to break that truce. Even if it was killing him not to tie her to her bed and keep her there until she promised never to take another risk on any guy she didn't know really, *really* well. The idea to hook up had been hers from the start and he planned to play by her rules until he could make her see….

What?

His pulse kicked up a notch as he tried to focus in on what he wanted. What last night meant. Being with Tori had been more than just a way to keep her out of trouble. He never would have slept with her if he didn't care about her. Because, damn it, he *wasn't* impulsive. He'd come here last night because he wanted her. Pure and simple. Not just for a night. Not just for a weekend.

Could he really want Tori Halsey for keeps? The thought blew his mind. Had this feeling been there all along? Lurking in his heart way back when? The realization floored him.

It also made him understand he needed to figure out what was happening before he drifted so far under her spell he'd never shake free. He needed to get out of here before the full import of what happened between them smacked him between the eyes. It wasn't only that he'd slept with his best friend's sister. It was his fear that he'd fallen for someone who lived a thousand miles away and hadn't expressed the slightest desire for anything more than a fling.

"Luke?" Her voice was throaty with sleep as she shifted in the hammock.

He couldn't deny a surge of longing at just the sound of his name on her lips. Still, he went through the motions of buttoning his shorts, a mild panic hastening his fingers.

"Hmm?" He searched for his shirt in the bushes and found it draped over a potted gardenia.

"You're leaving?" She dragged the bedsheet with her. At some point during the night he'd tugged it down from where it had draped over the porch rafters to cover her while she slept.

He'd never smell honeysuckle again without thinking of her and how she'd given herself to him so completely. If he hadn't known about the manhunt ahead of time, he would have never guessed she'd only been looking for a hook-up.

"I didn't think trophy men were supposed to stick around for breakfast." Wrenching the shirt over his head, he couldn't find it in his heart to regret the bite in his words. Still, he wiped it away with a kiss on her forehead. "You want me to carry you into bed before I leave? Are you cold?"

His light words didn't come close to capturing what he was feeling about her right now. Possessiveness surged through his blood like a virus. When had he developed feelings for her?

"I—" She shook her head. "I'm fine here. But I don't understand why you're racing out after all the times you told me I should take a relationship more seriously."

Ah, damn. If he knew the answer to that, maybe he wouldn't be running. Still, he thought through his response as thoroughly as if he had a key witness on the stand.

"After all the times you suggested I take a relationship *less* seriously, I thought it wise to play by your rules." He slid on his shoes, staying on the move lest he roll right back into the hammock alongside her.

She said nothing, surprising him. For the past week, she'd teased and tempted him, calling forth a response from him with suggestive conversation as much as the provocative pictures and clothes. So he didn't know what to make of her silence.

He had his shoes on, but couldn't make himself step off the porch. The torches still burned low, their flames dancing wildly in the breeze off the water.

"Right, Tori? I thought you were only looking for recreational sex."

"I thought so, too, but…" She bit off the words and shook her head.

"What?" His whole body tensed. Had being with him changed things for her? Hope sparked, even though he knew better than to have expectations of a woman who wasn't looking for anything serious.

"But last night felt like more than just sex. And I can't help but wondering if that's why you're jetting out at sunrise." Eyes narrowed, she stared at him like she was seeing him for the first time.

"I don't understand."

She pulled the sheet closer to her shoulders and drew near the edge of the hammock, her back straight.

"Back when you first kissed me, you said you knew there would be chemistry. You knew it from the very start, yet in all the years we've known each other, you never made a move. Maybe you avoided the attraction on purpose because you knew you'd never—" Shaking her head, she seemed to struggle for words. "You wouldn't have chosen someone like me."

"That's ridiculous." He wasn't sure he followed what she was trying to say. He also had no idea why she sounded so cool toward him just because he was trying to keep things uncomplicated—like *she'd* wanted.

"You have to admit, I wouldn't have exactly been the ideal girl for a guy intent on making partner before he turned thirty at a stuffy law firm. I've made a name for myself in the greeting card world as the woman with the sexy, over-the-top photos. But sexy and over-the-top hasn't ever described the kind of women you've dated. I'll bet your geologist girlfriend wasn't the impulsive type either."

Luke's brain finally began to follow. Sort of.

"You have to admit we're sort of polar opposites. But, yeah, I knew about the attraction. I even hit on you at my graduation party, but maybe you'd had too much to drink to remember—"

"Has it ever occurred to you maybe that's why you hit on me in the first place?" She bolted upright so fast the hammock swung behind her when she stood. "Maybe I'm just safer to have as a friend. I'm sure it was easier to make partner without a racy photographer showing up at the corporate Christmas party in a costume from the cavegirl photo shoot."

He blinked at the harshness of her words, knowing she was pulling this out of left field. Then again, hadn't he avoided stopping by Tori's place more than once when he was in town because he knew his attraction to her was unwise?

Suddenly, he was the one needing the hammock. He didn't like this view of himself one bit. From somewhere nearby, he heard something banging, reminding him dawn was approaching and people might be waking up soon. For that matter, their raised voices were probably being carried on the water.

"Tori, maybe you're right." He made a point of speaking softly. "But if I avoided acting on the chemistry between us, it was only to protect you from—"

Her chin trembled as her sheet blew around her. Tears glistened at the corners of her eyes.

Luke reached for her, but she shook him off.

"I don't need to be protected by you, okay? Not now, not ever." He'd never seen her so distressed, never would have anticipated touching such a nerve. "Just because I didn't choose a traditional path doesn't mean I don't know where I'm going. My family never understood that and if you can't see how damn well I've managed to protect myself—"

Behind them another loud *bang* caught them by surprise.

Instinctively, Luke pushed Tori behind him as he whirled toward the source of the sound.

And found one very pissed-off looking big brother glaring at them. Tim Halsey stood on the back porch, apparently welcomed by Daisy the black Lab, who wagged her tail next to him, oblivious to the guy's furious glare.

"Luke?" His longtime friend's voice broke through the soft sound of Tori's stifled sob. "I ask you to check up on my sister for me and I find her half naked and crying?"

He charged toward them, but before Luke could talk sense into him, Tori leaped out behind him to confront them both.

"You *were* only here to check up on me." She glared at Luke while keeping her brother away with a stiff arm.

Tim didn't seem to be pushing forward though. In fact, he eased back as the fierceness in Tori's tone became apparent.

"That's not the—"

"I asked you that on the first night when you showed up

with dinner." She swiped away any lingering hint of tears that might have been shed over him. "And you danced around the question, never admitting you were here because he sent you."

She shot Tim a scathing glance, too, and Luke sensed the end of any future with her unless he could talk his way out of it. Words failed him. No amount of law school had prepared him to fight for the woman he loved.

Yeah, *loved*.

He could see it now as plainly as the hurt and anger on Tori's face. He felt all that hurt and anger inside him, multiplied a few hundred times. The fact that he'd put that hurt there in the first place made it all the more devastating.

"There's more to it than that," Luke began, but she was already scooping up her clothes and running over the damp grass toward her small motorboat.

"What the hell is she doing?" Tim muttered, taking off after her, his boots making enough racket to wake the dead on the wooden porch planks.

"No." Luke held him back, knowing Tori would be furious if her brother interfered. "She can take care of herself."

"She's wearing a sheet and no shoes," Tim yelled, staring at him like he'd lost his mind.

But Luke knew he'd only just recovered it. He wouldn't stifle this woman ever again, even if that meant stepping back when all his impulses told him to take charge.

It took a hell of a lot of willpower to watch her yank the cord on the outboard motor of her ancient fishing boat and rev the engine to life. She sat straight in the craft like an old-time figurehead, taking on the world on her own terms.

"That's okay." Luke reassured himself even as he reassured his old friend. "Look at this place, will you?" He gestured to all the torches and flowers, the hand-laid stone path running up the lawn from the water and the paper lanterns. "She's not exactly living in poverty here. She's built a good life for herself since she left the farm, Tim. She's a smart lady who knows her way around the bay. She knows what she's doing."

Still, the realization burned his insides. Sure, he was glad to have recognized the inner strength Tori had cultivated against her family's overprotectiveness. But in admitting that she knew what she was doing, he had to face the fact that—just like she told him—she didn't need him.

Not now. Not ever.

SITTING ON A BEACH by the Pier near St. Pete's downtown, Tori texted her status for her friends, knowing they'd be curious about her plans for tomorrow.

Valentine's Day.

*No luck yet.*

Snapping a photo of herself seated on the sand next to a troop of squawky gulls, she uploaded the picture to her social networking page, figuring the upbeat visual would help prevent anyone from feeling sorry for her. She'd twisted the bedsheet into a toga after she'd roared away from Luke and her brother. She kept a life preserver and radio equipment in a locked box in the boat, so she hadn't been totally off her rocker when she'd taken off.

Although, she had to admit, perhaps her actions had counted as "flakey." She'd been at *her* house, after all. She could have just stormed inside and locked the door on both of them. But she'd been upset and not thinking straight. However, being on the boat always soothed her. She'd slid on her clothes once she'd gotten out on the water, a simple trick using her sheet to cover herself. Then she'd wrapped the sheet around her toga-style for an extra layer.

And for fun.

She'd e-mailed Tim from the beach shortly after sunrise

to let him know she'd call him later. Vaguely, she recalled him warning her that he would be down this month for a visit. But since the family visits—security checks, really—got under her skin, she'd put it out of her mind. Then, she'd been so absorbed with work and Luke, she'd forgotten all about it.

Luke.

She couldn't even think his name without opening a wound. Tim's Neanderthal behavior hadn't surprised her. That was why she lived so far from her family. But the fact that Luke only came around to check up on her at her brother's orders—now that *hurt*.

Her phone vibrated in her pocket and she fished it out, shaking a few grits of sand from the handset. When she opened the phone, she saw an incoming message with a photo attached.

Recognizing the image instantly, she straightened. Tensed. Hoped.

It was the e-card she'd done for CrownCraft's online division. The photo of the man and woman in the backseat of a cab.

The message with the card read:

*Although the woman in this photo doesn't wear a trench coat half as well as you, it sure is an artistically beautiful picture. I hope I can find the photographer to tell her how much I admire her talent. Her independence. And the way she looks in a toga.*

Tori stifled a half gasp, half laugh. Luke hadn't signed his name, but then he hadn't needed to. Her heartbeat sped madly as she peered around the beach for some sign of him. She didn't see anyone but a few early fishermen—none of whom were as hot as Luke.

Confused, she closed the e-mail and texted him back, grateful she was picking up wifi and good cell coverage.

*Where are you?* she typed, even though she was almost scared to find out why he'd felt a need to follow her.

*I'm on my way to the pier. I recognized the background from the photo you posted on your status page. Will you stay there long enough to talk?*

Was he being serious? She clicked back to her saved photos on the phone and saw the picture she'd snapped had plenty of landscape cues for a local. The buildings—the beach itself—would have tipped him off.

He hadn't followed her at all.

*Depends,* she typed, her fingers shaking a little so that she had to backspace and fix three typos in that one word. *Is my brother with you? I'm not letting him trick me into some shotgun wedding...*

After she typed it, she deleted every defensive word. She didn't want to bristle about old hurts done to her by the family or old regrets about not letting Luke into her life sooner. She simply wanted to see where a relationship might lead and if he was the man she'd dreamt he could be ever since he'd been her first crush.

Hitting the all-caps button, she simply typed *YES*.

How could she call herself a risk-taker if she didn't take a chance on love, even if she happened to be mad at her stubborn, overprotective lawyer?

Heart in her throat, she stood to walk toward the parking lot when the sound of a boat engine out on the water made her turn. She couldn't imagine how he'd arrived at the pier so quickly, but she recognized the boat even from far away. And not because of the expensive model or the distinctive catamaran hull that made it cut smoothly through the waves.

No, she could tell her lawyer had arrived by the red, heart-shaped flags whipping in the wind off his radio antennae. And by the ridiculously tacky and undeniably sweet wreath of red roses draped over the bow. He'd even brought Daisy, her black Lab. As they sped closer, Tori could see Daisy wore a pink bandana around her neck for the occasion.

Without saying a word, Luke was telling her he didn't mind her quirkiness and wouldn't care if she shot photos of cavemen in suede loincloths for a living. He'd made the most uncharacteristically splashy entrance she could envision for a staid attorney. That was, until he dropped anchor and jumped overboard, a rose clamped in his teeth like a lovesick pirate.

Giddy with laughter and flattered by such an extravagant display, Tori dropped her phone in the sand and ran into the surf to meet him. Legs slowing to a crawl once she got hip deep, she changed her approach and swam.

They met at the place where the water was shallow enough to stand but deep enough to cover them. Only then did she notice the water was freezing.

"What are you doing?" Shaking her head, she plucked the rose from between his teeth, freeing him to answer.

"I'm showing you how wrong you were when you said I didn't ask you out because I wanted someone more traditional like me." With a sweeping gesture, his arm came up out of the water to indicate the decked-out boat. "You see? I don't mind causing a stir. You have no idea the lengths I'm prepared to go to for you, Tori."

Water droplets beaded on his lashes, framing sincere eyes.

Touched, she felt the sting of tears in her own.

"I'm starting to figure it out." Her voice shook with the realization that Luke Owens was for real. Forever.

"And there's a small chance I overreacted about not wanting a protector."

He wrapped his arms around her, the warmth of his hands melting any reserves she might have had left.

"Is that right?"

"Who wouldn't want someone to help look out for them, especially if it means running interference with my family?"

"I know I wouldn't mind if you wanted to look out for me." His hands cupped her bottom and lifted her up into his arms so he held her in a bear hug. "I'm going to need a lot of help if I'm going to think about leaving New York behind to spend a lot more months of the year in Florida."

Her teeth quit chattering. Surprise and pleasure chased away any chill of the water.

"Really?" She kissed his face, all the more precious to her for the beautiful sacrifice he'd just offered to make for her sake. "Because I could probably spend some time in New York now and then. The city is still a fair distance from my parents' farm. I think we'd be safe."

He squeezed her against him.

"I wish you'd made that Valentine's Day pact a long time ago, Tori. I've needed you for a damn long time." The husky growl in his voice made her heart swell with soft emotions even as the rest of her melted against him.

"I've needed you, too. I don't know why I didn't see it sooner," she whispered against his lips before dragging her mouth along his in a tentative taste. "I was in such a hurry to distance myself from my family that I cut you off, too. Cut off whatever I might have felt for you."

"I wasn't showing up at your house every year because Tim told me to." His voice was serious now. His eyes intent. "The fact that he asked was just my excuse to see you again."

"I'm sorry I freaked out when my brother showed up. I was already panicking that you wanted to leave and my head was racing all over the place, not making sense."

"That's okay. I like thinking I can make you crazy sometimes." He grinned as he peered back at his flower-strewn boat. "Look how crazy you make me, woman."

Behind them, Daisy barked from the deck, the only Lab in history who didn't like getting wet.

"You sure know how to make a statement." She flung her arms wide and hugged him, so grateful to have this chance to make things right.

"I don't know that I can set a scene like a world class photographer, but I did my best."

"But how did you get here so fast?" she asked suddenly, knowing he couldn't have thrown all of this together at the spur of the moment. "With a Valentine's party in tow?"

"Well, first of all, I ordered the flowers and stuff for Valentine's Day a couple of days ago, knowing you really wanted a big romance blowout this year. So I already had all of this stuff at my place."

"You just happened to have all these roses on hand?"

"You can't hold it against me for being a planner as long as I don't hold it against you for…uh…making the occasional impulsive choice."

"Is that what you call my decision to speed away in the boat this morning?"

"You made a heck of a picture with the sheet whipping in the wind behind you." He molded his hands to her sides, the warmth of his palms penetrating the soaked cotton. "But to answer the rest of your question, I loaded up my V-day gear and set out into the bay, figuring I'd get a lead on a woman in a toga soon enough."

His hands slid under the sheet, reminding her that a deliciously happy ending to the day awaited her in the privacy of his boat. She happened to know he had a stateroom with a door that locked.

"You see? Aren't you lucky to be crazy about a woman who tends to be kind of memorable?"

"I'll never lose you this way," he acknowledged, his eyes

turning a darker shade as his hands cupped her bottom, urging her close to the hard heat of him.

"I'll make sure of it," she promised. Opening her lips to his, she sealed her commitment with a kiss to make Cupid blush.

* * * * *

# THE SATISFACTION
## Lori Borrill

To Betina and Joanne.
It was a pleasure and a treat to work
with such talented authors.

# 1

KITTY CLAYBORN stared out the window of Auntie Bea's Cards and Gifts watching a smiling couple stroll arm-in-arm down the boulevard.

"Oh, that's just wrong."

Jennifer, her part-time assistant, glanced up from a display of half-off porcelain Christmas angels. "What's wrong?"

"It's the day after New Year's. Everyone's supposed to be broke and hung over, yet this is the fourth couple I've seen going into Beekers in the past twenty minutes. It's not even the dinner hour. Will he really be as busy tonight as he is every night?"

Jennifer pulled the fifty-percent-off sign from the shelf and replaced it with one that upped the discount to seventy-five percent, solidifying the fact that Kitty would now lose four dollars on every one of the silly angels she sold—if she was lucky.

"I think it's great his restaurant's doing so well," Jennifer said cheerfully. "It's good for the neighborhood."

Right. And if even a handful of Josh Beekers' happy diners stepped into *her* store on occasion, Kitty would agree. Plenty glanced at her window displays before crossing the street, but their resulting looks of bland disinterest would make a herd of zombies seem like a lively bunch. She had to face the fact that, while the dwindling population of local farmers might love her country bears and sweetheart tchotchkes, the new wave of business flooding into town was looking for something else.

Something Auntie Bea's apparently didn't have.

In nightly droves, people swarmed into Shiloh, California, from as far as San Francisco, brought in by a riverfront revitalization effort that had turned the old dairy town into an upscale tourist destination. And while the rest of the community was reaping the benefit, Auntie Bea's was dying a slow and painful death.

"Beekers might be good for the neighborhood," Kitty grumbled, "but he's not doing anything for us. And if I don't do something to turn this business around, CrownCraft is canceling our contract."

Jennifer scoffed. "We've been their dealer for decades. I can't believe they'd drop us just because their bitchy sales representative didn't like the store." She stacked the last of the singing snowmen on the discount shelf next to the angels.

"Believe it," Kitty replied. "Andresen's Drugs has been trying to steal our account ever since Bea retired, and if I don't come up with a plan to boost sales they might get it."

Especially once the holiday sales figures went out. If CrownCraft hadn't been disappointed enough by her Halloween and Thanksgiving sales, they'd certainly be sharpening the ax once Kitty closed out her dismal year-end. And if they pulled her contract as an exclusive dealer for their greeting cards and stationery, she'd lose the only merchandise that was keeping her store alive.

It was obvious now that if she wanted Auntie Bea's to survive the store would need a complete makeover. But to what? That was the question.

Absently, she chewed on her pearl necklace, worrying over her situation as a group of women stopped on the sidewalk and waited to cross the street. One glanced at Kitty's window display, looking interested in something, but when the woman touched a finger to her lipstick, Kitty realized she was only interested in her own reflection.

Kitty's low mood sank further. "What are all these people looking for?" she mumbled.

"Huh?"

"These people who drive all the way up here to dine at Beekers. He draws in over a hundred customers five nights a week. What gifts could I sell that they'd come in and buy?"

Jennifer shrugged. "Why don't you ask Josh?"

*"Josh?"*

"Sure. He's the one talking to them all." Jennifer stepped to the window and eyed the restaurant across the street. Through the large picture windows the two could see the group of women being escorted toward the back of the dining room. "He spends half his night wandering from table to table chatting with his customers," Jennifer went on. "Haven't you ever noticed?"

Noticed Josh Beeker? Every woman with a pulse had an eye on that man. Ever since he'd brought that gorgeous cowboy body of his into town from Denver last May, he'd been stealing hearts. Most women swooned at the mere sight of him. He'd won the stronger ones over with charm. And if there'd been any left not desperate to spring naked into the man's big burly arms, he'd won those over with his award-winning menu. It was nearly impossible to be female and not take notice of Josh Beeker, and from Kitty's vantage point, she knew plenty of them had.

Kitty lived in the second-story apartment above Auntie Bea's, and often over the past six months she'd caught sight of Josh closing up shop for the night with someone tall and beautiful on his arm. She hadn't needed the rumor mill to guess that Josh liked his women the way he liked his wine— bold, smooth and full-bodied—three things Kitty wasn't. But that didn't stop her from drawing her shades and dreaming that someday she'd be one of those women, if just for one night.

Silly, since she could barely hold a conversation with the man without tripping over her tongue. Asking for his help with her store?

She took a deep breath and sighed. "That's actually a really good idea."

"Of course it is." Jennifer beamed. "*I* thought of it."

"I suppose I could go over and ask him to coffee." She toyed with the pearls around her neck. "Or I could ask him to stop by one night after he closes the restaurant. I do live right upstairs."

Okay, so that particular idea filled her head with so many fantasies she was sure she visibly blushed.

"Josh Beeker up in your apartment after hours?" Jennifer goaded. "I can only imagine how *that* would end up."

Kitty already had. In fact, her sex-starved mind had flashed past four erotic scenarios before she mentally jabbed herself back to reality.

Unfortunately, Josh picked that very moment to step into view as he brought a bottle of wine and that tongue-twisting smile to a couple seated at the window.

Kitty's heart skipped a little. Oh, the man was a meal for the eyes. He kept his sandy-blond hair cut short but mussed on top, perfect for accentuating a pair of beautiful green eyes the color of fresh moss. He was habitually tanned but for the pale circles around his eyes from the sunglasses he wore outside. He had that classic Colorado sportsman look, an adventurous cowboy without the drawl, with a bright white smile and full soft lips that made a girl want to kiss him. Or be kissed *by* him. All over.

But the pull that was Josh Beeker didn't come from his looks alone. The man had an aura, a special vibe that said wherever he stood was the best place to be. One got the impression life was good for Josh, or if it wasn't, he took his problems in stride. He oozed easy days and sensual nights, forever exuding the assurance that time spent with him would always be time well spent. And like everyone else, Kitty would love to catch a few of those sunny vibes for herself. If only she had the nerve to put herself in his path.

Unfortunately, she didn't. Because, despite all her yearnings and lusty thoughts, she was still the great-niece of sweet old Auntie Bea—too rural, modest and ordinary for a guy his friends called "The Beek." On Josh's wine list, Kitty would be grape soda, sweet and bubbly but nowhere near the piquant seductress that could compete in his league. But, oh, if things were different…

With a heavy breath, she sighed. "Okay, so maybe coffee *is* the best plan."

"If you've still got your sights set on Howard, I'd say so."

*Howard.*

Kitty groaned.

"Unless you've been keeping secrets," Jennifer added, "Santa never brought you a boyfriend and Valentine's Day is only six weeks away." She followed Kitty's gaze to Josh's restaurant across the street. "Instead of ogle-eyeing the town playboy, maybe you should start thinking about plan Howard."

Jennifer was right. After making the pact with Sam and Tori at last year's GCA Winter Trade Show, Kitty was determined to make her love life top priority. She'd spent much of her spring and summer dating a little, but mostly analyzing her choices in men and trying to get to the bottom of why, at the age of twenty-nine, she was still single with not an interesting prospect in sight. She'd concluded that her problem was that she picked men solely on the basis of attraction: case in point, Josh Beeker—dreamy on the eyes, sinful to the imagination, but a lousy option for anything involving futures, commitments and happy-ever-afters.

Yet she'd spent six months drooling over him, hadn't she?

Howard, on the other hand, was everything a wise, goal-driven woman would go for. Assistant manager-on-his-way-to-manager of the Shiloh branch of Hollies Paint Stores, Howard was a local, two years her senior, reliable, capable and intent on settling down with a house and family. And he'd been smitten with Kitty for as long as she could remember.

Howard was kind, *boring,* gentle and personable, *boring,* responsible and career-minded, *boring.* Everything she should be looking for in her quest for the long haul. Except—*okay!*—he was boring.

But that didn't change reality. Life with Howard had to be better than this endless string of going-nowhere relationships she always managed to stumble into. And who knew? Maybe if she gave the man a chance, she'd end up uncovering something special. So she'd promised herself that if she rang in this New Year just as alone as she had the one before it, she'd march down to Hollies and ask Howard on a date. No way was she going to be the lone survivor of the Valentine's Day pact, chugging down drinks in Chicago with Barry the Bartender while speculating what kind of wonderful, romantic evenings Sam and Tori were currently enjoying.

Just the thought made her shudder.

Of course, if she didn't have a plan to revamp her store, there wouldn't be a trade show for her this year. So putting thoughts of men and dating on hold, she turned her mind back to the business she sorely needed to save.

"You're right," Kitty announced. "Coffee it is." Definitely the safer bet.

Although, as her gaze lingered on the sexy man across the street, she wondered if, when it came to Josh, there was such a thing as safe.

# 2

"LADIES, I HOPE I can interest you in dessert." Josh set two plates on the table between the four women and began handing out forks. "This is a new dish we've been working on and I need some expert opinions."

The women eyed the two chocolate desserts with looks that said he wouldn't be twisting any arms.

"It's a chocolate espresso torte infused with raspberry liqueur, passion flower and something special I'm not giving away." He grinned. "I'm thinking about calling it Exotic Erotic Experience."

Vanessa, a stunning redhead around thirty with emerald-green eyes and a body that could stop traffic, was the first to take a bite. "Mmm," she groaned. Her eyes rolled back as she slid her tongue along her full bottom lip. "*I'd* call it Better than Sex."

Despite the wedding ring on her finger, Josh bent close and lowered his voice to just above a whisper. "If that's better than sex, darlin', I'd say you're sleeping with the wrong man."

He winked and the other three women roared with laughter.

"Maybe I am." She flicked her brows.

"Tell Tony he better get his game on or I might have to steal you away."

She slid a finger up his thigh then patted him on the ass.

"I'd better not. You know how hot-headed he is. You'd be buried in the cellar before I could lift a finger to stop him."

Josh feigned discomfort for the wife of his good friend, Tony Sacco, a winery owner out in Napa. "You're probably right. Let it be our secret."

"This is seriously good, Josh," said Alison, the thin brunette sitting next to Vanessa. "If it's not on the menu, it needs to be."

"That's exactly what I was hoping you'd say." He dipped a finger in the raspberry sauce and casually took a taste. "I think it's a keeper. By the way, ladies, dinner's on the house tonight. Can I get Marco to bring you coffee?"

Vanessa shook her head. "Oh, Josh, that's not nec—"

"I'll take it in trade for a free case of Tony's 2006 syrah next time you're in town."

She squeezed his hand in friendly affection. "You're the greatest."

He shrugged. "It's a curse, but I'm learning to deal."

Chuckling, he walked back to the kitchen of his restaurant thinking life didn't get much better than this. It had ended up being a winning move—following his parents out from Denver to California where they'd come to retire in the milder climate. A year ago, Josh had only flown out for a visit having no intention of leaving the restaurant he'd worked for since graduating from the culinary academy. But when he caught his first sight of Shiloh, he'd fallen in love with the area and decided to stay.

He'd bought up a prime location right on the main drag and hit pay dirt with a restaurant of his own that took off like a light and hadn't slowed down since. He'd brought a few of his friends out to help run the restaurant, had quickly made several dozen more, and was already considering himself a lifer in this slice of northern California that sat between the wine country and the Pacific Coast.

Especially if people kept offering up beautiful women like Vanessa and her not coincidentally single friends.

Sidling up next to Seth, his grill chef, he slapped two more chicken breasts on the fire.

Seth eyed Josh then focused his gaze across the dining room on the group of women Josh had just left. "If Vanessa's doling out friends, I'll take that blonde in the silky blue top."

Josh laughed. "That one's married. In fact, they all are except for the brunette in the green sweater. And Vanessa was subtle as a jackhammer about all the things Alison and I had in common." He checked his watch. "I'll be getting a call around ten tonight asking me what I thought of her."

"And what *do* you think?"

"Seems nice enough. As long as she understands the ground rules, I suppose I wouldn't mind spending a little time with her."

Seth placed a hand on his chest and sighed. "There you go breaking hearts across California just like you did back home."

Josh smiled and poked at the chicken he'd slapped on the grill.

Most of the wives of his friends had taken him on as their personal project, feeling the need to get him married off as though the future of mankind depended on it. They didn't seem to take him seriously when he told them he wasn't interested in settling down. They were all certain his mind could be changed if only he met that special someone.

And every one of them had a special someone in mind.

He'd told each of them more than once that it wasn't happening any time soon, but if they didn't want to listen and kept parading a string of eligible women in front of him, who was he to argue?

"The only heart I break is my mother's," he said. "And even she's happy now that Ginny gave her the grandchild she'd been waiting for."

The ring of the bell above the door caught his attention and he looked up to see his neighbor, Kitty Clayborn, step through.

Now, there was a woman he didn't quite know what to do with. Sweet, prim Kitty Clayborn. A curious paradox of buttoned-up propriety with hints of something dark and sensual underneath. He and Kitty had lived and worked in close proximity for over six months now, yet she still balled up like a bundle of nerves every time their paths crossed. He wondered what he had to do to get her to loosen up, to ease the chokehold she kept on that pearl necklace of hers, to take down that pretty blond hair and relax like he knew she could.

*Like she did after hours in that upstairs apartment of hers, late at night when the street was quiet and she thought no one was looking.*

He missed those hot August nights when she'd left her shades and windows open. Kitty had a fetish for smooth jazz, and often when he was closing up shop, he'd hear the sultry music wafting down from her second-story window. He'd never forget the first night he saw her up there, his straight-laced neighbor rolling her hips to the music in a pair of low-slung shorts and an even skimpier T-shirt. He'd gone rock-hard at the sight—still did every time he recalled it—and it was a situation he had yet to get a grip on. After all, he'd seen plenty of woman in his time dance around half-naked. So why did this one affect him so?

He knew the answer. That first hot and humid night, she'd shown him a side of her he hadn't expected, and ever since, he'd ached to see what else Miss Kitty might be hiding.

Unfortunately, that would involve asking her on a date, and if there was anything Josh knew about women like Kitty, it was that they didn't do temporary. And since Josh didn't do permanent that left only broken hearts and bad feelings among neighbors who live too close for comfort.

Clutching her purse tightly against her cashmere sweater, she eyed the room then smiled and waved when she spotted him at the grill.

"Hey, Kitty Cat," he called out. "You looking for a table?"

She stepped to the bar that overlooked the kitchen, set down her purse and took a seat. "No, thank you. I was looking for you."

He glanced back to find her fiddling with those pearls as though she were counting off beads on a rosary. The Billy Joel song came to mind, the one about only the good dying young, and Josh felt every bit the dangerous bad boy out to steal her virtues.

With pretty brown eyes, a lovely turned-up nose and angelic straight blond hair, Kitty oozed purity. Her family owned a dairy, which Josh assumed accounted for that fresh-cream skin and those luscious curves that couldn't be fabricated in a gym. Oh, what he'd give to get under that pale-blue turtleneck and unravel everything proper about his farm-fresh neighbor.

Anything but his bachelorhood, he had to remind himself.

"Actually," she said, clearing her throat, "I was wondering if you wouldn't mind having coffee with me sometime soon."

He grinned to hide his shock. "Why, Miss Kitty, are you asking me on a date?"

Just the thought turned him hard. Cute Sally Sunshine hitting on him? It was every naughty boy's fantasy. And every time he thought about him and Kitty getting naked, he felt like a deliciously naughty boy.

He seriously needed to get over himself when it came to her. He was bad news and she wasn't his type. End of subject. Yet every time he locked up the restaurant at night and headed down the boulevard, he couldn't stop himself from glancing up to those windows in search of a glimpse.

And now she was asking him out?

Those brown eyes turned to saucers and her rosy cheeks deepened. "No! Of course, not. I mean, not that I wouldn't be interested. Sure, a date would be fun—or not! That's not what I— I mean—" Her rosy cheeks darkened. "I need your help."

He left his chicken to Seth, who was doing a bad job of holding his snickers at bay, and leaned against the bar.

"You see, it's my store," she went on. "It's in trouble." Then in a babbling rush, she told him about Auntie Bea's and how her sales were sinking and something about a company named CrownCraft and a bitchy sales representative. Did she really say *bitchy?* Seemed funny coming out of her mouth. Regardless, she fluttered it out so quickly, he couldn't quite grasp it all, but what he did manage to get was that she wanted him to help her figure out how to revamp her store.

"I'm sorry," he said, when she finally came to a pause. "I don't know much about gift shops. I'm a chef."

"I…I know." Her hand went back to her pearls. "I was just thinking that your guests…surely, they must talk. Don't they ask you where they can buy things, where the good shopping is, or tell you what they're doing here in town?"

He blinked. Actually, they did. And when he gave it some thought, he realized he probably *could* give her some suggestions. Frankly, few people strolling into the restaurant would be interested in the antiquated kitsch she peddled. It didn't surprise him that she was running in the red. Did she know Auntie Bea's was sorely out of touch with the times? He'd just need to figure out a way to tell her that without hurting her feelings.

Or kissing her senseless.

"The restaurant's closed tomorrow. I'd have some time," he heard himself say. Then that worried brow of hers transformed into bright beams of sunshine that hit him smack between the eyes.

"Really?"

That smile literally wobbled his knees. Damn, he had it worse than he thought, which meant that if he was going to help her, he'd have to park his self-control in the garage and give it a great big tune-up.

She clapped her hands together. "Oh, I could kiss you!"

He'd never survive it.

"Don't get too excited," he urged. "I'm not sure if I've got any good ideas, but maybe I could help brainstorm."

She slid off the barstool and grabbed her purse. "I think you'll help more than you realize. Really. I've got a good feeling about this."

He had a feeling too. Unfortunately, the feeling was very, very bad.

# 3

"LOCAL ARTS AND CRAFTS?"

Kitty looked around her store as though she were trying to envision Josh's suggestion.

"Anything hand-made, one-of-a-kind," he said. "Especially things that are representative of the area or reflect the history of the town." He shoved his hands in his pockets and watched the little wheels turn in her head. "Like the stuff they sold at that Holiday Crafts Faire last November."

She darted her eyes to his. "I know the woman who organizes it. She also plans Dairy Days in the summer and the Art and Wine Festival in the fall. Between the three, I'll bet she'd have contact information on all the local crafts people in the county." Then her eyes lit up like a Christmas tree. "There's a quilt show, too. Three women in town make beautiful quilts. And one makes purses."

"Now you're thinking."

He followed as she circled the displays, mentally swapping out her inventory as she recalled the various things she'd seen at the shows.

"I could do this," she said. "It could work."

Those brown eyes were wide and excited, filled with hope and buzzing with energy. Kitty was normally so reserved Josh enjoyed seeing her vibrant and full of life. It was like getting a close-up view of the woman he'd glimpsed from afar.

"I could offer consignment," she went on. "That would reduce my overhead."

Her voice had taken on a musical tone that he found endearing. "I'm sure you could."

"And what do you think of the name?" She lowered her voice and blushed. "I've always wanted to change it."

"To what?"

"Cassandra's. It's my real name."

She threw the statement out casually, then stepped down the aisle as if what she said hadn't just slapped him up side the head.

Cassandra. It sounded like an alter ego, the woman who came out when the night was warm and the music was playing. The sexy, smooth-tempered blonde he was staring at now, the one who showed herself only after you made it into that special circle reserved for friends. Everyone else got Kitty: pleasant, demure Kitty who wore librarian sweaters and sold stuffed bears and porcelain cherubs to the Auntie Beas of Shiloh.

Sure, so she was only talking about a nickname, but something about the knowledge felt as if he'd been handed a clue to a mystery that kept getting more and more interesting as time went on.

"The name doesn't really fit the store as it is now," she added, toying with her knickknacks at the end of an aisle of greeting cards. "But if I did what you were suggesting earlier by going a little more upscale, I could easily see a name like Cassandra's working." She spun around and hit him with a smile. "Couldn't you?"

"Cassandra's a beautiful name," he found himself blurting.

Her cheeks reddened, but she looked more flattered than embarrassed. She smiled at the compliment, and then for a long moment, she simply stood and studied him.

Josh couldn't remember a time when he was at a loss for words. Most definitely never around a woman. But right now, he couldn't get a sound to form on his lips. It was mostly because he didn't dare utter what he was thinking. If he did, he'd tell her that her name wasn't the only beautiful thing about her. That rather unexpectedly, he was finding Kitty/Cassandra the most captivating woman he'd met in a long time. And that while his brain kept screaming at him to keep his distance, every other part of his body desperately wanted to get to know her better.

No. He couldn't say any of that. Not without the whole thing ending badly. So he just stood there looking dumb and stupid, trying hard to ignore the fire that crackled between them.

"Thank you so much for your help," she finally said, breaking the long silence. "You've given me some great ideas that I really think will work. I don't know how I can repay you."

Josh counted off five ways without even trying, but rather than open his mouth and casually spout them out the way he normally would, he held his tongue and forced out, "Don't mention it," instead.

She eyed the clock on the wall. "Come upstairs. Let me treat you to dinner."

"D-dinner?"

She quirked her brow and regarded him like the bungling teenager he'd suddenly turned into. "You do eat, don't you?"

"Well, yes."

"Did you already have other plans?"

"I, uh…no, not really."

Moving to the front door, she pulled a key from her pocket and locked up, shutting off his means of escape—not that he would have used it. This encounter was getting more intriguing by the moment. He was pretty much deciding on the fly that he should stay and let it play out.

She brushed past him, filling his nose with the sweet scent of vanilla and spice. "Come on back. The stairs are this way."

He watched those shapely hips sway as he followed her out the back door and toward the stairway that led to her upstairs apartment. Tiny voices in his head screamed off warnings, but he flicked them all back, reminding himself that dinner in her apartment didn't have to be anything more.

But when she turned around and grinned before starting up the stairs, the seductive look in her eyes said fat chance. He might be a little shaken up right now, but he knew a come-hither look when he saw one. Somewhere over the course of their conversation, his shy and tidy neighbor had gone firmly on the prowl, the shock of it freezing his feet in place as she began her ascent.

"Uh, Kitty," he said.

She stopped again and turned.

He scratched his head. "This is just dinner, right?"

A wicked smile curved her lips. "Is that all you want it to be?"

It was a trick question—one with no good answer. He could lie and say yes, that given their situation and his certainty that she didn't do flings, they would both be smart to keep their relationship purely platonic. But since when had he ever been smart? And more to the point, he wasn't entirely certain anymore that Miss Kitty wouldn't do flings. Thirty seconds ago, he would have said she'd never proposition a man on her stairs either, and look where he was standing.

So he opted for Bad Answer Number Two and told her the truth. "I'd love the whole night."

Her wicked smile darkened to something that got him hard. "Then come on." She took two steps up the stairs then halted abruptly when she realized he hadn't moved. "Is there a problem?"

*Say no. Just follow her upstairs and have the time of your life. Forget decency. Forget—*

"Kitty, we need to be clear," he blurted, shutting off his inner caveman voice. "I'm not a relationship kind of guy."

He expected a sorry look of disappointment, but instead Kitty simply smiled. "I'm not asking for one."

"You aren't?"

Turning, she stepped down two stairs so that her eyes were level with his and that pretty turned-up nose was mere inches from his lips. It took every ounce of restraint to keep from leaning out and kissing it. That was, until he glanced down and noticed how close her breasts were to his hands.

There was more of them than he'd given her credit for, most likely because she'd always buttoned them up under her white cotton blouses and cardigan sweaters. But today she wore a simple V-neck sweater, not low enough to show off cleavage but definitely tight enough to show she was packing some goods.

His hands itched to take hold of them, to cup them in his palms and listen to her breath hitch when he gave them a squeeze. He wondered what she looked like naked. Would her skin be lightly freckled or would it be smooth as satin? His cock twitched as he thought about it.

"I'll get my relationship from Howard," she said, jerking him from his fantasy.

*Howard?*

"But before I go down that road, I'd really like one night of pure, unadulterated fun."

He caught the smoky look of sex in her eyes and knew without a doubt that he could provide her with that—especially the unadulterated part.

*But who the hell is Howard?*

He had opened his mouth to ask when she turned away and headed back up the stairs, that shapely ass of hers pulling his mind off Howard and back to that thing she said about not expecting a relationship and just wanting fun.

Josh liked fun. And he had no doubt that if he followed her up those stairs, he'd find lots of it. So, not needing to be asked twice, he took them two by two, anxious to see how many more surprises this strange day was going to bring.

## 4
_____

WITH TREMBLING FINGERS, Kitty opened the door to her apartment, stunned by disbelief that she'd actually propositioned Josh—and more shockingly—that he was still behind her, apparently interested in what she'd offered.

Did she have any idea what she was doing?

Not a lick.

In fact, she'd officially stepped so far out of her element she was walking in uncharted territory. Without a map. Or a compass. Or a tank of badly needed oxygen.

She and Josh were supposed to have gone out for coffee after she closed her shop, but when he'd shown up and they'd started talking, everything had gone off course and hadn't steered back yet. He'd started rattling off ideas for transforming her store as though he'd given it serious thought, which she'd found not only impressive but adorably sweet. He'd gotten her excited, had her not only buying into his ideas but had pointed her straight to the place where she needed to start. Her worries and fears for her business had begun to dissipate. Hope and promise had taken their place.

And then she'd turned to see him looking at her as if she was the most desirable creature he'd ever laid eyes on.

A little voice in the corner of her conscience had screamed to take a chance. A sure and comfortable future for Howard and her would still be there next week. But before she opened that door, she should grab one wild fantasy night with the man she'd been lusting over for half the year.

To her shock she'd opened her mouth and suggested it. To her thrill—and mortification—Josh Beeker was actually here ready to provide it.

Pushing the door open, she stepped into her apartment and glanced over her shoulder. "Come on in. I've had chicken stewing in the slow cooker all day."

Not that eating sounded very appealing at the moment. She'd made the comment only to keep her mouth moving, sure that if she didn't she'd freeze up completely.

"It's a recipe that comes out similar to a coq au vin but with half the effort. I hope you like it."

Josh closed the door and raised a brow in intrigue. "You sound like a cook."

"I'm no graduate of the CIA, but I hold my own." She set her keys on the kitchen counter and reached for two glasses. "Would you like a glass of wine?"

"I'd love one."

He leaned against the counter as she pulled a bottle of chardonnay from the refrigerator, poured two glasses and handed him one. "This is a treat," he said. "I don't get cooked for very often."

"No?"

"Most people are intimidated."

"Why? Are you picky?"

He laughed. "Not in the least, but people assume I am because I'm a chef. I can sometimes talk my mom into making me her meat loaf, but even that's been ages now that they're retired and on the go all the time."

"How awful."

"It is." Taking a generous sip of his wine, he set it down and moved in close, entering her space and setting all her nerves on alert. "I lead a very sad and tortured life."

The edge of his mouth turned up into a teasing smile as his gaze roamed over her face, upping the heat in the room and stifling the air between them. That look had come back to his eyes, the hungry, appreciative glance he'd taunted her with downstairs. Except now it was up close, magnified and packing twice the punch.

"I wouldn't go that far," she managed to utter.

He feigned disappointment. "You don't believe me?"

"I live across the street, remember? You seem to be having a good time of it."

Tracing a light finger along the edge of her jaw, he shook his head. "Ah, but I can think of a couple of things that would greatly improve my disposition."

She swallowed. "Like?"

"For starters, this."

He bent in and touched his mouth to hers, just a simple brush of the lips, a tentative taste that from anyone else might be mistaken for a sweet friendly peck. But this was Josh. Her late-night fantasy man whose touch sizzled all the way to her toes.

She sighed and eased into him, flattening her palms against his chest, feeling the beat of his heart as he moved closer and added pressure. A moan slipped up his throat, a sound that spoke of surprise and unexpected pleasure, and for a moment, he kept it simple, kissing gently then easing back to study her eyes, her face, her lips.

Then those green eyes darkened.

With a curse, he pulled her against him, closing his mouth over hers and devouring her as if she were one of his sumptuous desserts. One by one, her muscles lost their strength. Her brain went fuzzy, seduced by his strong arms and drugged by his taste, the heady mix of oak and berries and something uniquely male. It stole her breath and teased her senses, leaving her hot and wet and aching for more.

"What are you doing to me?" he whispered, but he didn't

seem to want an answer. Instead, he backed her against the counter and moved his attention down her neck, smoothing his tongue in light circles toward the sensitive spot under her ear. He nudged his hips against her and she gasped when the sharp bulge of his erection pressed against her waist. She wanted to feel it unimpeded, experience the solid length of it filling her and stroking her wild. Her body yearned for it so badly she nearly sobbed.

This was everything she'd dreamed of, exactly the image that had filled all those fantasies over so many nights. She'd known Josh was a passionate man. He couldn't whip up food so sensuous without living and breathing emotion, and forever, she'd ached to see if that same level of heat followed him into the bedroom.

Finally, tonight she'd find out.

"This thing you're doing," she urged. "Please don't stop."

"Darlin', I couldn't if I tried."

Then in one swift move, he grabbed the hem of her sweater and yanked it over her head, unclipping her bra and sending it to the floor right after.

"Oh, help me," he said, his voice low and hoarse and full of need.

The sudden surprise of baring herself to him gave her the fleeting urge to cross her arms over her chest, but it was lost the moment those big warm hands slid over her breasts and gently squeezed.

He bent low and touched his tongue to one sensitive nipple, lighting a fire deep in her belly that had her squirming for release even though they'd barely gotten started. Would it be an embarrassment to come to orgasm fast or was it a compliment to the chef? Kitty didn't know. Before now, it had never been an issue. But as he began sucking and caressing her senseless, she came within inches of finding out.

She tried to stay focused, gliding her fingers over the

spiky strands of his hair, listening to his gentle whispers of pleasure and appreciation. But just as she thought she might have found her groove, he muttered, "I need more," and slid her slacks off her hips as well.

"Take this off," he said, pulling her panties down to her knees and tugging off one heel.

"But—" she started, and the rest of the sentence stuck in her throat when he gripped her butt and pressed his mouth straight between her legs.

She heard something low and appreciative, realized it had come from her, and clasped the cool tile for support. If he wanted this to be over, he'd chosen the quickest and most direct path. But just as she felt the first surge come over her, he tempered his activities and moved his focus down her thighs.

"It's too much," she managed to say.

He only grinned, flashing that sly wicked smile she'd seen in her dreams so many nights. "There's no such thing as too much."

Gripping her waist with his hands, he hoisted her onto the counter, the frigid tile on her butt doing nothing to chill the heat pooling around her. Then he parted her legs and smoothed his thumbs over her clit.

He hissed in a breath and groaned. "You're so wet."

"Do that again and I'll come," she warned. But instead of fending him off, it seemed to act as an invitation.

"I'd like that very much." He slipped a finger up her core and swallowed hard when her muscles gripped him.

"I don't think that's such a— Ohhh…" A second finger followed, halting her protest as pure pleasure rolled through her.

He resumed the light kisses, pushing his fingers in and out and stealing her will to fight it. The feeling was too glorious, the man too talented. So she lolled her head back and let go.

"That's it," he said, upping the pressure as her breath shortened and her toes curled. "Come for me, babe."

With every touch of his lips another surge ran through her, running deeper and lingering longer as he moved in closer. He lightly bit at her sex, sucking a gasp from her lungs that quickly morphed into a moan. And then, as if she could handle more, he parted her folds and swept his tongue directly across her clit.

She climaxed instantly, her heels striking the cabinets as the blinding energy took hold and didn't let go. Pulse after pulse ripped through her, an orgasm so endless she feared something was wrong, until she realized her lover was still in control, lapping, stroking and torturing every final wave out of her. From somewhere in the distance she heard his pleasured whispers, each thrust of her climax echoing back with his sounds of ecstasy until it drowned out with a final sigh.

Sliding back onto her elbows, she closed her eyes and calmed her breath as Josh's groans eased to kisses and his kisses eased to a light feathery touch.

"Have I mentioned how beautiful you are?" he asked.

She opened her eyes to see him studying her with that dark and sensual look in his eyes.

She smiled and lazily nodded.

"Then I can say you're even more beautiful naked and flushed."

The fog cleared and she blinked, sitting back up and suddenly very aware of her sprawled legs and vulnerable state. "Oh, my word," she began. "This wasn't supposed to— You haven't even—" But Josh simply laughed.

Wrapping an arm around her waist and the other under her knees, he lifted her from the counter and stepped to the edge of the kitchen.

"Darlin', that was just an appetizer." He eyed the only hallway off the main living area and started off in that direction. "Point me to your bedroom and we'll get to the main course."

# 5

WITH KITTY IN HIS arms, Josh stepped down the hallway horny and hard and wondering how things had gotten so hot so fast. He'd never let a kiss get so immediately out of hand. He could only imagine what Kitty must be thinking.

*Ask The Beek to come in for dinner and in ten minutes you're naked and crying out your first orgasm.*

Classy, Josh. Real classy.

He'd only intended to go for a kiss. He'd wanted to find out if these sparks he'd felt between them were just a product of his fantasies, set to fizzle the moment he had the real thing in his hands. He'd half expected it to turn out that way, had attributed his interest in his neighbor to the forbidden-fruit syndrome—the appeal of taking something he shouldn't have as opposed to real desire for the woman herself.

Only, when he'd held her in his arms and locked lips with hers the sparks didn't fizzle, they exploded. And now he was caught in a bonfire, not sure where this night might end.

"That one," Kitty said, pointing to the last room on the right. He'd thought for sure he'd walk in and find a frilly bedroom stuffed with silk flowers and antique dolls. Instead he found a four-poster bed dressed with a quilt and packed with so many sinful ideas he nearly turned around in search of the couch.

He was going to need more than one night.

He set her on the bed and began unbuttoning his shirt as Kitty went to work on his jeans, her eyes growing wide when she pulled down the fabric and his stiff cock sprang out before her.

She gaped. "It's so…big."

He looked at himself then at her. "Darlin', you definitely know how to stroke a man's ego."

"But it is," she said plainly.

He started to spout out something about merely being average but the words froze in his throat when she palmed him and took the tip into her mouth. What felt like a speeding freight train swept through him, jerking his hips and lunging a curse from his mouth.

"Oh, babe, you better not—"

"Mmm, I like it," she said, positioning herself square in front of him then using her other hand to cup his balls. "Besides, I think it's your turn."

He stood rooted in amazement as he watched his sweet humble neighbor take him into her mouth and lick him. This, the woman who'd tripped over her words practically every time they'd exchanged greetings, the one who worried over her pearls, who wore cute embroidered chinos and sold little porcelain farm animals to old ladies in mom jeans. His sweet Miss Kitty was now sucking him off like a seasoned pro. If that wasn't the ultimate wet dream he didn't know what was.

His heart pounding in his chest, he touched his fingers to her soft silky hair. "Oh, babe, that's incredible."

"You're so hard." She pressed her lips to the base of his shaft and began kissing a path to the tip.

Each touch pumped a burst of pleasure straight through him, pushing him further toward the edge and sounding off alarms when she circled her tongue around his cock and gave it a long slow stroke. He had to close his eyes to keep from exploding, and when she added a soft massage to those sensual kisses, he had to pull from her grasp and take a step back.

"I'm hard enough," he said, his voice strangled as he worked to hold on. His jeans still hanging from his waist, he reached into his back pocket and took out a condom. "Let's move the party."

And then he was on top of her, sheathed and stiff and aching for the sweet taste of her smooth curvy body in its entirety.

Slowly, he eased inside, giving her tight space time to adjust while he tried not to notice the sexy flush to her cheeks or the way those dark-chocolate eyes had turned all naughty on him. But his traitorous brain made him peek, and what he saw nearly broke him in half.

Oh, help him, she was beautiful, aroused and relaxed and sprawled across her bed like an angel with wings. He pushed in the rest of the way and began a steady stroke, watching as her breath hitched, as a shimmery glow coated her beaming face, as she ground and begged and bucked and finally came apart around him. And when she did she took him with her, flailing him into a climax so sharp he literally cried out for mercy.

The whole experience shook him, leaving him dazed and wondrous and not quite sure of himself. Josh liked sex. And he'd had plenty of it in his adult life. But this time had been different. Different how, he didn't know, but when he collapsed on the bed and cradled her in his arms, he couldn't deny the feeling that he'd just wandered into something deep.

She lazily stretched her arm over his chest and sighed. "That was amazing." Then she gave him a sleepy smile. "Promise me we can do that again before you leave."

He forced a smile, his gut instinct alternating between the urge to flee and the desire to stay. But when he opened his mouth, he heard himself say, "Anything your heart desires, babe."

"THIS IS DELICIOUS," Josh said, and not just to be nice. As he sat at Kitty's table digging into his second helping of slow-cooker coq au vin, he tried to remember the last time he'd been treated to a simple home-cooked meal. Probably not since he moved to California, for sure.

"I'm glad you like it," Kitty said. "It's a recipe I stole from my mother's card file."

Using perfect table manners, she cut off a small slice of chicken and took a dainty bite. With her clothes back on she'd returned to the prim and polite woman who'd sweetly greeted him in Auntie Bea's, only now her nervous edge was gone, and more enticingly, Josh was well aware of the sinful sex kitten that lurked underneath that proper facade.

Which made her an even hotter turn-on, aided by the fact that though she'd dressed and combed her hair, that pretty face still revealed the glow of a woman well-sexed and sat-isfied.

He took a bite of his meal then washed it down with a gulp of wine. "Despite all my years in cooking school, I find the best recipes are still those we steal from our mother's kitchens. Running the restaurant, I don't get enough of it."

"Does that mean you're willing to try my mother's famous tuna casserole with the potato chip topping?"

He quirked a brow. "You make tuna casserole?"

"No." She laughed. "I was being facetious, though my aunt Elena does make a delicious Tater Tot casserole with hamburger, sour cream and canned mushroom soup. It's a heart attack on a plate but well worth the risk."

"I'll take you up on that one." He chuckled and popped a pearl onion in his mouth.

Kitty was funny. When had she gotten funny? And why hadn't he seen hints of any of this during all those months he'd worked across the street? It was as if every assumption he'd held about her was coming up wrong, and before the night was through, he wondered how many more surprises she'd have in store for him.

Which brought him to the question that had been bugging him for hours.

"So, who's Howard?" he heard himself ask before his brain could fully deduce whether doing so was a good idea.

She didn't so much as blink.

"Howard Bloombauer, the assistant manager down at Hollies Paints?" She waited for him to recognize the name but he'd never been in the paint store. "I guess you've never met him."

"Are you, um—" how did he ask this? "—dating?"

Her eyes widened. "No, of course not. If I were, I wouldn't be here with you."

"I didn't think so, but earlier you'd said something about Howard and a relationship and…"

With a casual shrug, she started in with something about spending her Valentine's Days at a trade show and some pact she'd made with two friends about not ending up dateless and alone this year. That took her into a long history of her dating experiences which, while not lengthy, had involved a couple of relationships that ended up going nowhere. That led her to the subject of Howard.

If Josh understood it all correctly, she'd been leaving the poor schmuck waiting in the wings for her to take an interest, marry him, pop out a few kids and live happily ever after. She'd given herself a deadline and if something better didn't come along before that date she was going to resign herself to a life as Mrs. Bloombauer—*Kitty Bloombauer?*

Josh's part in all this was to show her one glorious last hurrah—her proverbial bachelorette party, it sounded like— which, she'd very appreciatively admitted, he'd provided with honors.

She'd made the whole thing sound completely logical and

sane, though when he retraced it in his mind he couldn't quite get the pieces to come together so nicely.

"So to keep from spending another Valentine's Day stag in some bar in Chicago," he asked, "you're planning on marrying Howard?"

"Well, I'm not exactly going to *marry* the man." Her eyes bulged as though hearing it put so plainly had her seeing the absurdity in it all. "I was only going to ask him on a date and see where it went. But yes," she said, reaching to her neck for the pearls that she wasn't wearing anymore. "I admit that much of Howard's appeal is that he's a man interested in settling down and having a family."

And Josh wasn't.

He got the picture. But why it gave him a sour taste of insult left him totally baffled. It was true he wasn't interested in settling down, at least not right now. So hearing his lover accepting that fact should have him thrilled, not put him off. It was confirmation that he genuinely didn't have to worry about this evening creating problems between him and Kitty. After all, they were neighbors and neither of them planned on going anywhere soon. Though he'd believed her when she'd said she was only interested in one night of fun, he knew through experience that sometimes what a woman said and what they meant were two different things. He should be relieved to hear her confirm that she wasn't expecting anything from him, that in all assurance, he could go home tonight and not worry about losing their neighborly friendship.

So why wasn't he grinning with joy?

"It sounds like you've got a good handle on your future," he mumbled awkwardly. Then before he could stop himself, he spouted out, "There's a beautiful art center up in Mendocino. Would you like to go check it out?"

She looked as surprised as he felt. "With you?"

He frowned. "Yeah, with me. Next Monday would be best since the restaurant's closed. Can you get away from the store? The gallery gift shop is exactly the kind of thing I had in mind for Auntie Bea's. We could drive up and make a day of it."

He'd planned none of this before this very moment. Yes, he'd thought of the art center and had considered mentioning it to Kitty. But making it a date hadn't been part of the equation until the thought of the impending Howard had Josh securing his place with Kitty for at least a while longer.

And the stupidity in that was something he had no intention of analyzing any time soon.

"Sure I can." She grinned. "I haven't been to Mendocino in years. I'd love that. Thank you."

"Good." He nodded. Then, before he had a chance to spout out any more bright ideas, he decided to give his mouth an activity that was far less likely to get him in trouble.

Rising from the table, he stepped over and took her hand. "Let's go back to bed."

# 6

"WHAT DO YOU THINK?" Josh stood in the center of the Mendocino Art Center gift shop holding up something that looked like a cluster of ceramic mushrooms with faces carved in the caps.

Kitty wrinkled her nose. "What's it supposed to be?"

"Who cares? It looks strange, unique and expensive. That's all that matters."

She took a tentative step toward it. "The faces look evil." Frowning, she turned to a display of colorful silk fish hanging from a large branch of driftwood. "Can't I sell these instead? I love these, and I could have them in the store without fearing they'll come to life and haunt the place at midnight."

Josh laughed and set the strange piece back on the counter. "Darlin', you can sell anything you want."

The woman behind the counter chimed in. "The fish are actually amongst our bestsellers."

Kitty gave Josh a victorious smirk, prompting him to step close and tap a playful finger to her nose. "Don't get cocky on me."

He held his eyes on hers long enough to fill her spine with tingles and heat her veins. Oh, the man was handsome. And she'd gotten to see plenty of him in the week since she'd first invited him up to her apartment. Since then, every night after he closed the restaurant he'd made an excuse to stop by, which had inevitably led them to the bedroom, which inevitably led to seven straight nights of soul-bending sex. She'd formed a fast appreciation for those sizzling looks and that easy smile that seemed poised to spring out at the slightest prompting. But even more devastating was when that free-and-easy gaze of his darkened to something deep and sultry the way it did sometimes when they made love.

*The way it did right now.*

It was a look that reached out to her irrational side, making her think about silly things like love and futures. It was foolish, she knew. But she'd been foolish all week, allowing Josh to come to her apartment bearing treats from his restaurant and sharing her bed as if she were a woman who knew how to pull off a temporary fling. Kitty was a forever kinda girl toying around with a man who wasn't a relationship kinda guy. And if she didn't get some strength back into that tingling spine of hers, she was headed for nothing but heartache.

Clearing her throat, she took a step back and flashed her best noncommittal smile. "I'm not cocky, just well-trained. You've done your job well. I appreciate your bringing me up here and showing me around all the shops and galleries." She held up her BlackBerry. "I've managed to gather a long list of artists and some great ideas for the store. I really owe you one. This arrangement has ended up being far more than I'd expected when I'd first sought out your help."

She blinked and diverted her gaze from the truckload of innuendo loaded into that comment. She'd wanted it to sound like the goodbye speech she needed it to be, one that would put an end to their week of fun and frolic. But instead of taking the bait, he waved her off and talked her into a walk on the beach before heading back home.

Strolling the Mendocino shoreline in the dead of winter wasn't one of Kitty's habits, but as she'd been discovering all week, when she took Josh's lead, wonderful things happened. Thanks to the brisk weather and overcast skies, the beach was deserted and the resulting solitude was relaxing. For more than a mile, they walked the stretch of coast without running into another soul, chatting out stories of things they'd done and places they'd been. And when they got to the end where the rocky cliffs jutted out to the pounding surf, they stopped and stared out over the ocean.

Though Kitty hadn't been shivering, Josh opened up his big flannel jacket and tucked her inside with him, nestling her against his strong chest where her head cradled perfectly into the crook of his shoulder. A secure warmth smoothed over her, fueled by the feel of his heartbeat against her fingertips, his gentle breath against her cheek and his drugging scent that had become so deliciously familiar. She cinched her waist against his hip and held tight, letting the pounding surf fill her ears while his gentle caress stoked her senses.

"Your cheeks are pink," he said, lifting her chin with his thumb and forefinger. "Are you cold?"

"Not when you hold me like this."

Then he smiled at her with those devilish eyes and pressed his full lips to hers. He stroked her mouth with his, brushing tenderly. It was a tentative taste, a gentle sampling of flesh and a mingling of pleasures. She loved that he kissed this way, slow and steady, as if he could linger for hours in the pool of her breath. Prodding her open, he slipped his tongue toward hers and circled it in a sensual dance that ramped up the heat and sent it spiraling toward her womb. It pulled a moan from her throat and sent her swooning against him, dizzy in the luxury of that tall hard body pressed against her.

Oh, why couldn't this last? she wondered. Why was it that the men she liked best were always the ones who had other plans for their futures? Kitty was seriously beginning to believe that when it came to men she must be cursed, banished to an eternal purgatory brought on by some past sin she was unaware of. And basking in the company of this fun, passionate soul she began to feel angry. Life wasn't fair to give her a taste of something so joyous only to know it was destined to end. It was a terse reminder that she wasn't cut out for flings, and that today she needed to end this game of chicken she was playing with her heart.

As casually as possible, she pulled from the kiss and rested her cheek against his chest. "It's beautiful out here," she said, making sure her tone was light.

He took a long breath and exhaled. "Yes, it is. I always thought there was nothing more stunning than the Rocky Mountains. Looking at them, you're overcome with the power of nature. It's humbling and inspiring all at the same time." He lightly stroked her shoulder. "I get that same sensation here at the ocean, only more so. It's one of the reasons I fell in love with the area. While I love the mountains, I've always been a water boy. So much so that I'm considering moving onto my boat."

She glanced up at his face. "Really? Your boat is that big?"

She'd known Josh kept a boat at the marina, a cabin cruiser with a bed and kitchen. Though she'd never seen it, she hadn't gotten the impression it was big enough to sub for living quarters.

He shrugged. "I've been talking to a few of the people who live on the marina. The weather's so mild here people seem to get along fine. Since I eat most meals and do all my entertaining at the restaurant, my apartment isn't of much use to me these days. The bathroom on the boat is small, but I could easily add a nice shower at the restaurant then save all the money I'm dumping into rent." He shrugged again. "It's just something I'm considering since I spend the bulk of my free time on it anyway."

"It sounds…exciting."

And of course like clockwork her mind quickly sped to the thought of Josh abandoning his apartment for hers instead. He wouldn't need to put a private bathroom in the restaurant or live on his boat. He could live with her, right across the street from his restaurant, and keep the boat for recreation. They could spend their days off sailing down the river toward the bay, or—

She gave herself a mental douse of cold water. What was she thinking, taking a casual comment and warping into a fantasy life of cohabitation on land and sea? She must be deranged, especially considering he'd flat-out told her to expect nothing in the relationship department.

And she supposed if they'd left it at that one blissful night, she would have been fine. But they hadn't. He'd come back for more, again and again. And now the weak and feeble shield she'd placed around her heart was beginning to feel the strain.

This was it. She needed to get out while she had the chance. But as she plotted her Dear Jane speech she heard him ask, "How would you like to go for a cruise on my boat sometime?"

"Your boat?" she muttered.

"Yeah. It's nothing fancy, but the river's gorgeous in the morning when the sun comes up. Could you get Jennifer to cover for you one of these mornings? You could spend the night and we could eat breakfast with the egrets."

Breakfast with the egrets. Chilly romantic walks on desolate winter beaches. Art galleries, delectable dinners, sumptuous desserts. Not to mention the simple pleasures of campy movies by her fireplace followed by mind-blowing sex on her living-room rug.

She'd lived more this week than she had in a lifetime, which was exactly why she needed to open her mouth and say thanks, but no. Any more of this and she'd never settle for Mr. Hometown Howard. And if she couldn't settle for Howard, that meant continuing on in her life without prospects, cursed by the fact that her desires forever exceeded reality.

But to her own dismay, she glanced up, took one look at those charming green eyes and all her wits and senses hit the highway.

"I'd love that," she said. "Yes, that would be nice."

# 7

"I HAVE a confession to make." Kitty stepped down the stairs to the cabin of Josh's boat. "When I first saw this boat, I thought you were crazy to want to live on it. But now that I've spent some time here, I realize there's really a lot more space than you'd think."

Josh followed her down and tossed himself on the queen-size bunk. "I've got plenty of space." He spread his arms across the bed. "There's even room for two here."

She started to wash the breakfast dishes, apparently not picking up on his hint. "And really," she went on, "the more I think about you living on a boat, the more I think it suits you."

"And how is that?"

"It's adventurous and fun, and—" She paused over the sink and considered. "*Mobile,* I guess is the word that comes to mind." She looked at him and grinned. "No roots."

He frowned. "I've set roots in my restaurant."

"Yes, that's true. Though I think more metaphorically than literally there's something wanderlust about you, and living on a boat seems fitting." She caught the look in his eye. "Don't get offended. I'm paying a compliment. I think it's exciting to be with such a free spirit. Years from now I can tell my grandchildren I once had a sordid affair with a charming sailor back in my youth."

She chuckled and Josh should have laughed with her. Her

comments were innocent enough, but something about them struck a chord. He wasn't sure he liked the label of wanderlust sailor. It didn't fit the image he had of himself. And he *knew* he didn't like the idea that someday in the future what he and Kitty were sharing would only amount to a distant memory of a sordid fling. Something about that seemed…dismissive, only when he turned it all over, he couldn't find a single point to argue.

So maybe he had always insisted on putting his personal goals and aspirations in front of the old ball-and-chain. He'd never wanted to be saddled with responsibility he didn't need. But did that really make him nothing more than a mere trophy on some woman's bedpost?

The question got sideswiped when Kitty pulled off the old Broncos T-shirt she'd borrowed, displaying that sweet curvy body in all its naked glory, and reached for her bra as if she planned to get dressed.

"Hey, what are you doing?"

"I've got to get to the store."

He slid off the bunk, tugged the bra from her fingers and covered her breasts with his palms instead. "It's early still." Then he started trailing kisses from her shoulder to her ear. He'd learned over the past two weeks that it was the quickest way to get her thinking what he was thinking. And right now, going to work wasn't the thought on his mind.

Her lips curved into a smile and she closed her eyes. Her head lolled to the side. "I suppose I don't have to leave right this moment."

She moaned when he moved the kisses down to her breasts. He loved how responsive she was, how every touch from his hand resonated through her and surged back through his fingertips. It was instant gratification, and it created a delicious cycle of give and take that he'd come to crave.

He lowered his voice and spoke close to her ear. "I treat

you to breakfast on the river with a beautiful sunrise and flocks of ducks and egrets and this is how you repay me?"

"Well, I—" Her words faltered when he cupped his hand between her legs. "Don't want to seem ungrateful," she finished with a sigh.

"That's my girl."

Tossing off his shorts, he led her toward the bunk and crawled into the cozy space, pulling her on top of him, where she straddled his waist. She quickly took to task, pressing her lips to his chest and circling her tongue around his nipples, caressing his body with that glorious combination of touch and taste. It never got old, watching his frank and mannerly lover morph into a wanton seductress when he got her into bed. Nor had it stopped getting him rock-hard.

He ran his hands over her silky skin, tracing those curves while her gentle moves and hot kisses pumped his body to life. And when he slid a finger into her slippery heat his cock twitched and jerked with demands that it take over.

"Ohh," she groaned. "You always know right where to touch me."

When it came to Kitty, everywhere was the right place to touch her. But he kept that to himself, opting to let her believe he had some magic power. In reality they just made a really good team.

He reached into one of the compartments, pulled out a condom and sheathed himself, not ready to sink in yet but getting closer by the minute. Every press of her mouth, each easy stroke of that butt against his cock turned the dial up a notch until the temperature in the room reached a boil.

Grabbing her hips, he nudged her so that the length of him stroked against her clit, then he urged her to rock and massage herself against his shaft.

"That's it, babe," he said, holding his penis to up the pressure. "Stroke like this."

She did, grasping his shoulders and sliding back and forth until those brown eyes darkened and her rosy cheeks flushed.

"Ooh, this is nice," she moaned. Her long blond hair slipped over her shoulders and tickled his cheek. After a night of sex and a morning of cruising on the calm glassy water she looked tousled and mussed. Her makeup was smudged, her normally tidy hair hung haphazardly around her shoulders, and her fresh soapy scent was laced with sweat and sex. To Josh it was the ultimate turn-on, the unraveling of something pure that he wasn't sure he'd ever get enough of.

Pulling back, she raised her hands and clasped the porthole over the bed, stretching out that long body of hers where he could watch as she moved and stroked over him. It nearly broke him, watching her go from pleasure to ecstasy to urgent as the pressure built and she reached the edge.

Her breath deepened. "Inside," she urged.

"Not yet." He ground his hips, upping the rhythm. "Come for me, babe."

She moved her focus to the spot where their bodies met, taking slow and deliberate strokes and then speeding up the pace until that faint squeak began to lift from her lungs.

"It's here," she urged. "It's—" But the words drowned out with her climax.

The second she came, he pulled her up and buried himself into that tight pulsing space. Her muscles squeezed and quaked, thrusting him from aroused to the edge of orgasm in only a few strokes. He began pumping hard, drawing out her pleasure as he reached his peak. She threw her head back and cried out, riding the waves as far as they would take her, pushing into him, churning over him, until everything exploded.

He came hard, wrapping his arms around her and dragging her to his chest, flipping her over on her back so he could take control. It nearly devoured him, the fierce desire and greed, the carnal ache to pillage and possess. It raked the air from his lungs and the light from his eyes, leaving him nothing to do but surrender himself as his body spilled and thrust.

He came to rest against her, his mouth pressed to her warm, sweaty cheek, his face crushed against hers and her body wrapped within his arms. Short of his heavy breath and the soft caress of his lips, his muscles were too spent to function. And yet, despite everything he'd given his mind to concentrate on, no matter how numbing this round of magnificent sex, he couldn't stop harking back to Kitty's comments.

*Distant memory of a sordid affair, my ass.*

He'd had fond recollections of women before. There were several notable evenings keeping hold in his memory banks. But his experience with Kitty overshadowed them all. And as much as it shouldn't, he couldn't stop being bugged by the notion that this deserved something more notable than a melancholy tale from a gray-haired lady.

This was special. And it was really, really good. The problem was he wasn't at all prepared to deal with what it *should* be.

# 8

"THE CROWNCRAFT rep is thrilled with my ideas for Auntie Bea's," Kitty said, holding up the Inventory Clearance Sale banner she'd made while Jennifer taped it to the window.

"You mean Cassandra's?" Jennifer corrected.

Kitty smiled. "She even liked the name change. She'll be up in the area next week and wants to talk about swapping out their inventory for products that will be more suitable for the new store."

She stepped back to check the sign. "I guess, for a while at least, I'm out of hot water with them."

"So you'll be going to the trade show."

"Booked my plane ticket yesterday."

"And will you be staying for Valentine's Day?"

Kitty eyed her friend, not missing her look of insinuation.

"I saw Howard the other day," Jennifer added. "He asked how you were doing."

"And you said?"

"I didn't tell him you've been sleeping with The Beek, if that's what you're wondering."

Kitty frowned. "You don't have to lie. My relationship with Josh is no betrayal to Howard."

"Is that what it is? A relationship?" Kitty didn't have an answer, prompting Jennifer to add, "Valentine's Day is only a few weeks away, you know."

"I know what day it is, I've just been—busy."

Jennifer picked up the stepladder and carried it to the storage room. "Busy whiling away your nights with yet another man who will get you nowhere. *This* one even told you on day one not to expect a relationship." She sighed and eyed Kitty pathetically. "Tell me you don't actually think that situation's changed."

For two weeks now, Jennifer had been warning Kitty about getting too involved with Josh, reminding her that it was supposed to have been a one-night stand. It wasn't that Jennifer didn't like Josh. It was that, for ten years now, she'd been on the receiving end of Kitty's romantic frustrations and broken hearts. She'd listened to hours of sobs and woes and was the brainchild behind the idea of Kitty using her head instead of her heart to find the man of her dreams, since the other way around hadn't gotten her anywhere.

"No, I don't," Kitty confirmed. "And you're right. Wasting my time with men like Josh is exactly what's left me single and pushing thirty. And, no, I haven't given up plan Howard. I just—"

She just hadn't wanted to let go of the wonderful time she was having, or the sexy way Josh made her feel, the way her tummy tingled every time she set eyes on him, how he touched her, the passion in their lovemaking, that he could make her laugh at the slightest things, or—

Kitty had to sit down. Plopping onto one of the crates they'd been emptying, she wrapped her arms around her waist and groaned. "Oh, no. Jennifer, I've fallen in love with him."

Jennifer stood and stared. "What?"

"I knew I had it bad, but not as bad as this."

"Kitty, Kitty." Jennifer's tone was chastising, as if Kitty were the stupidest woman on earth, and she couldn't argue. She'd played with fire and something had ignited. What had she expected?

And worse, it only proved that Kitty had a serious problem

when it came to men. After all, if it weren't for Tori and Sam and the pact they'd made last year, Kitty wouldn't even be considering Howard right now. She would have continued this fling with Josh indefinitely until he ultimately tired and broke her heart. And how much more of her life would she have wasted while she watched more of her friends marry and start families?

No, she wasn't going there. She was going to stick to plan Howard, give the guy a solid chance, and if things didn't work out between them, she'd at least know it wasn't because she'd made another stupid mistake.

"I need to break it off with Josh," she said.

Jennifer eyed the restaurant across the street. "Now would be the perfect opportunity."

"He's busy. I can't bother him at work."

"He's never too busy to chat with customers. He'll make time for you."

"But—"

"Kitty, I know you. You're a softie and a sucker for charm. If you get him in private, he'll just talk you out of it. Don't you remember Ron?"

Ron was a distributor whom Kitty had managed to get involved with a couple years back. On a biweekly basis, the man waltzed into town, wined and dined her, talked business, had sex, then headed back to Los Angeles until next time. Over and over again, Kitty had intended to break it off, but he'd kept stringing her along with stories about how he was thinking of relocating to the area. Until, of course, he took a job in New York and was gone forever.

"Yes, I remember Ron." She sighed and stared out the window. "You're right. I need to start making better choices when it comes to men, and I need to start now. I'm going over there, and as soon as I'm done, I'm walking down to Hollies Paints and asking Howard on a date."

She stood and smoothed the creases from her slacks. "One big swoop before I can change my mind and back out."

"Go," Jennifer urged. "Plan Howard was a good one. He's a nice guy and I really think that if you gave it a shot you'd find something special with him."

Kitty had already found something special with Josh. *That* she knew all the way to her soul. But without two sides to that street, she was only headed for another dead end on her road to something lasting. So, with her chin up and her shoulders squared, she headed over to Beekers, determined to do this before she lost both her heart *and* her nerve.

She walked in and found him at the grill. "Josh, can we talk?"

He turned around and his face lit up. She tried not to let the sparkling smile affect her, but with three weeks of blissful memories running a slide show in her brain, she couldn't help feeling a solid lump in her throat. And it didn't help that he was standing there in those sexy chef's whites that broadened his shoulders and trimmed his waist. No wonder the women fawned all over him when they came into the restaurant. With the delectable smells sizzling off the grill at the hand of the mouthwatering man creating them, all the senses were plundered and no female was left with a fighting chance.

"Hey, it's my favorite gift-shop owner," he chimed. "What can I do for you, darlin'?"

She swallowed hard and shored up her will. She'd have all the time in the world to feel sorry for herself when this was done. Right now, she had to grow a stiff spine.

"I know you're busy, but we need to talk. It'll only take a moment."

The other chef at the grill eyed her then Josh. "Sounds serious."

Josh's smile turned inquisitive. "Sure." He grabbed a towel and wiped his hands as he rounded the bar. "What's up?"

"Could we talk in private? Maybe out back or—"

"Follow me."

He led her to a storeroom, where he turned on the lights and shut the door. "What is it, babe?"

"I, um…" Her fingers found her pearls and she began toying with them nervously. "I don't mean to do this suddenly, but this—relationship—we've been having." She waved a finger between them. "This thing between us—this, well, you know."

He crossed his arms over his chest and waited for her to keep going.

She cleared her throat. "Anyway, Valentine's Day is coming up, and if you remember my pact with my friends at the trade show."

Then in a rush everything she'd told him that first night in her apartment came spilling out. She sounded more like a kid explaining a broken lamp than a grown woman taking control of her love life, but it didn't matter. She was conveying the message somewhat coherently, and Josh was getting it, judging by the way his bright mood darkened and his lips went flat. Most likely, the man had never been broken up with before, and though Kitty garnered no pleasure from that notion, it helped to explain the sorry look on his face.

"Plan Howard," he said, his voice flat and unadorned.

"You have to understand. There are things I want in life that you don't. The years are getting away from me. I'll be thirty next year, and I can't go on indefinitely waiting for a lasting relationship to simply present itself."

He shook his head and agreed, "No, you can't."

"I just—I wish I could be like you, happy with my career and my friends. If that were the case, I'd take you for as long as you'd have me. But I'm not. I want a husband and a family and stability, and—" Her voice hitched and she had to stop. And thankfully, by then, Josh didn't need to hear anymore. Instead, he pulled her into his arms and gave her a warm hug.

"Babe, I understand."

That was good. Maybe he could explain it to her. Because despite what she'd said, she really didn't accept why, when two people had such a wonderful and intimate time with each other—who seemed to connect on so many levels bringing such pleasure to each other's lives—why that wouldn't be something a person would want to hold on to forever. She certainly wanted it. But apparently Josh saw things differently.

Maybe what was a spectacular relationship to her was only run of the mill to him. She'd been across the street long enough to know that after her, a dozen other women were no doubt lined up, waiting for Josh's attention. So what would be his motive to settle for a simple townie like her?

She pulled from his embrace and threw on a phony smile. "I'm glad." She took an awkward step back. "I can't tell you how much I appreciate everything you've done for me and my store. You're a good neighbor."

*And a good man, and lover, entertainer, chef, friend, confidant—*

"It's been my pleasure," he said quietly.

His face was smiling but there was something hollow in it. Nonetheless, she wasn't in a position to stay and analyze. She'd almost managed to get through this without completely humiliating herself in at least a half-dozen ways, so she needed to get out while she was still ahead.

"I'll see you around then?"

"You know where to find me."

Then without another look, she scampered from the room, through the restaurant and into the chilly evening air, gulping a breath and telling herself that after pulling off that stunning performance, she should be capable of just about anything.

# 9

"THAT WAS SOME speech, man."

Josh jumped at the sound of the voice behind him before remembering the couch in the back of the storeroom and the fact that Nick, one of his prep cooks, often napped there while waiting for his wife to come pick him up.

Great. Now, not only was he shocked and sad, his love life would be public knowledge.

"So was that good news or bad?" Nick asked.

"Come again?"

Nick shrugged. "When a guy's getting dumped you never know if the woman's tearing him apart or doing him a favor. So which is it?"

Josh blinked. "I'm not really sure."

Gut reaction? Kitty Clayborn had just taken his heart and put it through a meat grinder, seasoned it with arsenic then handed it back to him on a platter. But experience had taught him that having a woman do the breaking up was always a good thing. It was clean and easy. No hard feelings. A virtual get-out-of-jail-free card in the game of life. Besides, in the past, usually by the time they'd done the dumping, Josh had already moved on.

Except this time he didn't have any desire to move on. And this time, it didn't feel anything like a good thing.

"I vote for doing you a favor," Nick said. "'Cause that

woman's so in love with you, if it weren't for this deal she made with her pals, you would've been screwed."

Josh frowned. "What are you talking about? She never said anything about love."

"You've got to read between the *lines,* man."

Josh stared at Nick—a hippie, thirty years Josh's senior—and wondered if all those drugs the guy had done back in the sixties had finally caught up with him.

"All the stuff between the lines," Josh repeated flatly. "And you managed to catch all that from behind the canned tomatoes?"

"I only heard what I heard. But take it from an old guy who's been dealing with women since before you were crapping in diapers, that was not a girl happy about breaking up with you."

Dismissing Nick's assumptions, Josh frowned and headed back to the kitchen, his heart aching and his head too confused for cooking, but he tried anyway. Burying himself in his work had always been cleansing. When problems arose, he'd always used the job to take his mind off things and adjust his attitude long enough to step back and see answers clearly. Only tonight, no answer came, and an hour later, all he'd done was burn two game hens, yell at his favorite server and spoil a batch of ziti.

This wasn't right.

No matter how he turned it over in his head and tried to make sense of it, he kept coming back to the same place. That the breakup wasn't right, his reaction to it wasn't right, and plan Howard was a disaster waiting to happen. But dammit if he could sort through the clutter and make sense of how this *should* have panned out.

He kept going back to the same thing: for Josh, marriage wasn't an option. He knew that fact plain as day. Hell, he'd been repeating the phrase that he wasn't a relationship kind of guy for fifteen years. So, remembering that, and considering that it was the only thing Kitty wanted, he should be thrilled and relieved she'd ended it. Except he wasn't thrilled. Instead—in all irony—he felt as caged and trapped as he had that day so many years ago when the prospect of marriage and family had nearly ruined him.

Josh had only been nineteen, just starting fresh in the culinary academy with a bright future ahead of him and world-famous instructors telling him he had everything it took to hit it big. Then his girlfriend—the love of his life— turned up pregnant, and suddenly school and bright futures and hitting it big disintegrated in front of him. Instead he faced a dingy apartment, a crap job that barely paid the bills and the stark realization that said girlfriend wasn't anything close to the love of his life.

To his relief it had only been a false alarm, and in all his thanks and glory, he'd been able to keep the life he'd dreamed of, but the situation had changed him forever. He got real religious about birth control and put his brain firmly in charge of his heart. No one would be able to take his dreams away, and never again would he mistake lust for love.

Simple. End of subject. And for fifteen years, it was.

Only now, the memory of that frightening situation did nothing to ease the anxiety in his chest or the panic running through his veins. Now, the thought of losing Kitty gave him the same sense of dread he'd had back when he'd feared losing his career.

How did he explain that?

*You know what it is,* said a voice in his head. *You're losing something you desperately want. Hurt is hurt and need is need. Only this time it's a woman, not a career.*

He stared at his grill, at the diners in his restaurant, at the staff bustling to keep it all going. This was everything he'd ever wanted and now he had it. And unlike those early days, having a relationship on top of it wouldn't threaten to take it away. He really didn't have to choose between a family and a career anymore. He could have both. In fact, with Kitty he could have both rather nicely, if he could just get over the terror he'd been harboring for half his life.

That was the problem. The terror. The sheer unbending fright of leaving the safety net he'd shrouded himself in for so long. Even though everything in his gut said Kitty was special, that what they had was special, and that he'd better grab on to it before it slipped from his hands, those fears had become so ingrained, they'd become part of who he was.

Was he really capable of flipping the switch just like that?

He tossed down the tongs in his hand and muttered to Seth, "I've got to get out of here."

"You sure?" Seth asked. "I've got some grilled tuna I thought you'd like to burn to a crisp first."

"Oh, that's hysterical."

"No, what's hysterical is seeing you brought to your knees by a woman." Seth eyed Josh sympathetically. "She must be pretty great."

He'd gotten that right. Kitty was definitely pretty great. Now, what was he supposed to do about it?

SHE'D GOTTEN THE HARD part over with and she'd made it out in one piece. As Kitty stood in front of the glass doors of Hollies Paints, she told herself the rest was downright easy. Just walk in, ask Howard on a date and walk out. Then her duty would be done, her future would be set properly in motion, and she could go back to her store and spend the rest of the night in tears.

*What a perfect thought with which to greet the man you might spend the rest of your life with.*

Taking a deep breath, she worked to pull herself together, reminding herself that she wasn't marrying Howard. This was just the beginning of a relationship that might actually go somewhere for a change, that was all. Just a small step forward, and if it didn't work out, she'd end up a little wiser and go from there.

It was enough reassurance to have her grabbing the handle and opening the door. She walked into the bright lights as the happy door chime announced her arrival, and from behind the back counter, she spotted Howard in his blue Hollies Paints polo shirt.

Howard was a pleasant-looking man with a sunny disposition. Tall and gangly as a teen, he'd grown into his body over the years, and now those blue eyes seemed almost a little sexy under the dark bangs on his brow. She hadn't seen him in a while, and her memory kept straying back to those gangly teen days. Looking at him now was a nice surprise. He was better-looking than she'd remembered.

*Yeah, but could you* do *him?*

She almost visibly gasped at the devilish thought that sped through her, but it brought a badly needed smile to her face. She surely couldn't go up and ask a man on a date looking as though she'd just lost a bet.

"Hi, Kitty!" Howard said cheerily. "What brings you here? Going to give the store a new look? I heard you're making some changes down there."

The heavy boulder she'd felt in her chest began to ease. Howard really was very sweet.

"No, actually." She stepped to the counter then eyed left and right, checking to see who might be listening and happily finding no one around. "I came to see you."

He grinned. "Lucky me."

*Yeah, lucky Howard.*

She shut her conscience down before it got in the way of her goal and blurted, "I was wondering if you'd be interested in going out with me sometime. Soon."

The happy look on his face vanished. "You're asking me out?"

"Yes." She opened her mouth to expand on that, but the only thing that came out was another, "Yes."

He smiled awkwardly and scratched the back of his neck. "Gosh, that's really flattering, Kitty, but…I've already got a girlfriend."

She froze. "A what?"

"Yeah, I'm kinda dating someone."

"Dating *who?*"

Okay, so she didn't need to sound so astonished, but… well…she was astonished. This town was small. Mrs. Marney down on Broad Street didn't change her cat's litter box without half the town knowing about it. Howard Bloombauer getting a girlfriend? That would have made the *Shiloh Gazette*.

"Yeah, for a couple of weeks now. She's an interior designer who had the booth next to mine at the Sonoma County Home Show a while back. She just bought the old Baker house, came in for paint and, well…" He smiled victoriously. "We're dating now."

"You're dating now," she repeated, the words trailing off to a whisper as she stared into space and felt her future glide away from her.

"Sorry," he said. "Maybe if it doesn't work out—"

Pasting a quick smile on her face, she gave him her congrats, mumbled something about seeing him around sometime and walked out the door, trying hard to process everything that had just happened.

Somehow, in the span of fifteen minutes she'd thrown away the best thing that had ever happened to her, showed up a day late for the man who would save her future, and placed herself squarely in the company of Barry the Bartender come Valentine's Day.

If there was ever a time to start crying, now would be it.

# 10

"I'M A FOOL. I got exactly what I deserved."

Kitty wiped a tear from her cheek as Jennifer handed her the box of tissues.

"You need to stop being so hard on yourself." Jennifer returned to pulling boxes down from the storeroom shelves as Kitty sat useless at the dinette table, feeling sorry for herself and watching her friend work. "It's not your fault that things turned out the way they did."

"Yes, it is." Kitty blew her nose then tossed the tissue in the trash. "I was greedy. My mother always warned me about being greedy. I had the bird in the hand, but first I wanted to play around with the bird in the bush, too. And what happened? I lost them both. I deserve everything I got."

"Come on, Kitty. Howard barely dated for ten years. Who would have thought the man would find a girlfriend two weeks before you went after him?"

Kitty only shrugged, not daring to admit to her friend that what had her so upset wasn't losing Howard. It was ending things with Josh. In all honesty, once the shock had worn off, a side of her had breathed a sigh of relief when she'd walked out of Hollies Paints. As nice as Howard was, she really wasn't interested in the man. And having him rendered unavailable excused her from having to go down that path.

No, what had her in tears and kicking herself was that she'd idiotically broken it off with Josh when in the end she hadn't needed to. There she'd been, enjoying some of the most wonderful times of her life with the dreamiest man she'd ever encountered and she'd ruined it for nothing.

Yes, so the relationship was going nowhere. Yes, she might have gone along with it indefinitely, wondering if he might change his mind about commitment. Who knew for sure? Maybe given enough time, Josh might have come around. Maybe if she'd only given them the chance he might have started feeling about her the way she felt about—

She groaned and buried her face in her hands.

Listen to her. *Maybe Josh would have come around?* How many times did she have to get burned by that kind of thinking before she wised up? Josh wasn't going to come around. He'd made that clear from the first day. So instead of moaning over the loss of their relationship, she should be thankful she'd got out when she had.

She only wished it didn't hurt so much.

"I hate my life," she said, not liking the pitiful words or tone but too exhausted to care. Besides, it was the only way to sum up the gut-wrenching sadness that had started as soon as she'd admitted she was in love with Josh Beeker and had culminated at this very point. Her life sucked. There was no way to sugar-coat it.

Jennifer sighed. "Try not to be so down. I know this seems bad, but try to accept the fact that you and Howard simply weren't meant to be."

"I'm not meant to be with *anyone*. That's the problem."

"Oh, of course you are. Somewhere out there is the perfect man for you. You just have to try to stay positive and believe that he exists. He's out there."

"Out where?"

"How about right here?"

The sound of Josh's voice in the doorway gave them both a start and Jennifer yelped and placed a hand to her chest.

"Sorry, ladies," he said. He held his eyes on Kitty's. "You must not have heard the bell."

Kitty blinked. "Josh, you're—"

For a split second, she wondered if he was a wishful figment of her imagination. After all, he was dressed exactly as she'd left him in his chef's whites and jeans.

She glanced at Jennifer, who tossed her gaze between Josh and Kitty. "Then again," Jennifer said, "maybe the perfect man is the one both of us least expected." She cleared her throat and glanced at her watch. "Oh, look, it's closing time. I've got to get going." Brushing by Josh on her way out of the storeroom, she added, "Don't worry about closing up. I'll get the lights and lock the door on my way out."

And before Kitty could even process what was going on, the showroom went dark, she heard the jingle of keys and the slam of the door.

She stared at Josh. Had he really said what she thought he'd said?

The faint beginnings of a smile curved his lips. "So, you're in the market for the perfect man, are you?"

She wanted to answer, but her emotions were quickly closing the tight space around her throat. Between the sight of those sizzling green eyes and the seeds of hope sprouting in her chest, it was all she could do to breathe. So she nodded, trying not to let her expectations run away from her before she could fully understand what he was doing here.

"Well, I'm nothing close to perfect," he said. "But I'd like to apply for the job."

"You—" The word came out in a whoosh. She sucked in a breath, her heart pounding so fiercely that the blood was rushing from her brain and making her dizzy. Or maybe causing her to hear things?

"I have a prep cook who seems to think you love me," he

went on. "If that's true, then I should at least have the guts to tell you that I love you back."

New tears welled in her eyes, except these weren't tears of despair. They were tears of joy. Okay, she hadn't misunderstood. Josh had really come after her, he was really standing here, and he'd just said—

"I do," she managed to utter. "I do love you."

That half smile broke into a full gleam. "So the old guy was right."

It took him three steps to bridge the gap between them, to scoop her up and pull her into his arms.

She choked out a sob as his strong arms encased her, wrapping her in the warm embrace she'd thought she'd never feel again. Her body didn't know whether to melt against him or clutch him hard and hold on tight. She was still in shock, not quite certain where this was going and giddy over the words she'd heard.

Love? Had he really used the word *love*? And to Josh, what exactly did that mean?

She lost her contemplation when he closed his lips over hers, caressing her cheek with the lush warmth of his breath, tangling her tongue with his and filling her ears with the sweet music of his moans. They kissed and kissed, neither of them willing to break this connection. She craved the taste of him, ached for the heavy feel of his body in hers, and when he finally pulled back and cupped her face in his palms, her body mourned the loss.

He stared into her eyes, studying, searching. "These weeks have been some of my best times ever." He touched a gentle finger to her cheek. "When I'm with you, I feel I've got something special, something good that needs to be held on to and explored. I don't want to break up."

"I don't want to either."

*Ever.*

Then taking a small step back, he took her hands in his. "Then you'll go tell Howard you've changed your mind."

She sniffed. "Howard's apparently got a girlfriend."

"That's convenient. Saves me from the prospect of having to kick his ass."

She giggled. "You're not the violent type."

"Love can drive a man to do all kinds of things." Then he swallowed and added, "Like marry a woman, if that's what she wants."

Her mouth fell open.

"*Marry* me."

Was this seriously a marriage proposal? She might believe it if it weren't for the raw fright she saw in his eyes.

Releasing his grip, she took two steps away, wanting to pull herself together. This was wonderful. It was amazing. It was her most precious dream coming true. But it also wasn't right.

"Josh, I'm not looking for a marriage proposal," she said. "I just want to be with someone who's willing to take that step someday when the time is right." She didn't want to ruin this beautiful moment, but still she knew she had to get this straight. "You said you weren't a relationship kind of guy. It's not right to force you into something you don't want."

Some of the tension in his eyes eased. "Babe, I've been holding on to fears that lost their meaning years ago. There was a time when I didn't want commitments, and over the years it just turned into my way of life. But you made me realize that I'm not that guy anymore." He took a step closer. "I do want roots, here in this town with my restaurant and with you."

She touched a hand to her lips. "You really mean that?"

He moved in and pulled her close. "Darlin', you're the woman I want. This is what I want. And if you're going to be telling the grandchildren stories of sordid flings with wanderlust sailors, I plan to be there making sure they hear my side of it."

She lost her breath, but she didn't need it. Her blood pumped with life from those sweet words. "Oh, Josh."

"I'm in love with you, and I'd like to see where we can take this wonderful thing we've got going."

He took her in his arms and lavished her with kisses as reality seeped in and filled her heart. So she hadn't needed to choose between love and the life she wanted. She'd found a man who both excited her and offered stability all at the same time.

She pulled back and caught her breath. "I only have one condition."

"Name it."

"I need a date for Valentine's Day."

He grinned. "Darlin', you've got one for the rest of our lives."

# *Epilogue*

"You owe me fifty bucks."

Manny waltzed into the bar, late for his shift as usual.

"I don't owe you anything," Barry insisted. He slapped down cocktail napkins for two suits at the bar, filled their glasses with the house draft and snatched up their twenty.

"Oh, yes, you do, buddy boy."

"For what? I already told you I wasn't taking that bet on the Superbowl."

Manny gestured around the bar, pointing to the pink and red streamers and flicking a finger at a dangling lace heart. "Don't you know what day it is?"

"Uh, let me guess. Valentine's Day?"

"Yet the bar is missing three beautiful women we'd come to count on over the years."

Only when Manny pointed to the empty table in the corner did Barry remember the three ladies who came in every year for the Greeting Card Association's Winter Trade Show.

Barry frowned. Crap. Okay, so he *had* forgotten. And, yes, he had made the bet with Manny last year that the women would be back. And, yes, the table was empty. But— "It's early still. They'll be here. You aren't winning any bets until closing time."

"Actually," Manny said, "I'll take my money now. This was left for us at the front desk." He plopped down a flowery card decorated with hearts and a half-naked baby on the front holding a bow and arrow.

"What's with the kid?"

"It's cupid, you moron." Manny picked up the card and handed it to him. "Just read the card."

Inside was a perky "Happy Valentine's Day" followed by the handwritten inscription:

Dear Barry,
Sorry to break the news to you, hon, but this year you'll have to pay up. We've all got dates this Valentine's Day so we won't be by for drinks.
Better luck next time.
XOXOXO
Tori, Samantha and Kitty

"Son of a—" Barry slapped the card down on the counter.

"I'll take it in cash." Manny held out his hand and grinned like the cat that ate the canary.

Barry hated when Manny won a bet. As if losing money wasn't bad enough, the man had a habit of rubbing it in that Barry could do without.

"Not so fast," he said, not willing to part with his hard-earned cash without putting up a fight. "See the three blondes at the end of the bar?"

Manny followed Barry's gaze. "Yeah."

"They're here every Saturday night. Double or nothing they're still here come Memorial Day."

Manny eyed the women for a long time. "Memorial Day, huh?"

"Double or nothing."

With a reluctant huff, Manny held out his hand. "All right, buddy boy. You've got yourself a deal."

* * * * *

*Rancher Ramsey Westmoreland's temporary cook
is way too attractive for his liking.
Little does he know Chloe Burton came to his ranch
with another agenda entirely....*

That man across the street had to be, without a doubt, the most handsome man she'd ever seen.

Chloe Burton's pulse beat rhythmically as he stopped to talk to another man in front of a feed store. He was tall, dark and every inch of sexy—from his Stetson to the well-worn leather boots on his feet. And from the way his jeans and Western shirt fit his broad muscular shoulders, it was quite obvious he had everything it took to separate the men from the boys. The combination was enough to corrupt any woman's mind and had her weakening even from a distance. Her body felt flushed. It was hot. Unsettled.

Over the past year the only male who had gotten her time and attention had been the e-mail. That was simply pathetic, especially since now she was practically drooling simply at the sight of a man. Even his stance—both hands in his jeans pockets, legs braced apart, was a pose she would carry to her dreams.

And he was smiling, evidently enjoying the conversation being exchanged. He had dimples, incredibly sexy dimples in not one but both cheeks.

"What are you staring at, Clo?"

Chloe nearly jumped. She'd forgotten she had a lunch date. She glanced over the table at her best friend from college, Lucia Conyers.

"Take a look at that man across the street in the blue shirt, Lucia. Will he not be perfect for Denver's first issue of *Simply*

*Irresistible* or what?" Chloe asked with so much excitement she almost couldn't stand it.

She was the owner of *Simply Irresistible*, a magazine for today's up-and-coming woman. Their once-a-year Irresistible Man cover, which highlighted a man the magazine felt deserved the honor, had increased sales enough for Chloe to open a Denver office.

When Lucia didn't say anything but kept staring, Chloe's smile widened. "Well?"

Lucia glanced across the booth at her. "Since you asked, I'll tell you what I see. One of the Westmorelands—Ramsey Westmoreland. And yes, he'd be perfect for the cover, but he won't do it."

Chloe raised a brow. "He'd get paid for his services, of course."

Lucia laughed and shook her head. "Getting paid won't be the issue, Clo—Ramsey is one of the wealthiest sheep ranchers in this part of Colorado. But everyone knows what a private person he is. Trust me—he won't do it."

Chloe couldn't help but smile. The man was the epitome of what she was looking for in a magazine cover and she was determined that whatever it took, he would be it.

"Umm, I don't like that look on your face, Chloe. I've seen it before and know exactly what it means."

She watched as Ramsey Westmoreland entered the store with a swagger that made her almost breathless. She *would* be seeing him again.

*Look for Silhouette Desire's*
*HOT WESTMORELAND NIGHTS by Brenda Jackson,*
*available March 9 wherever books are sold.*

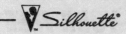

# SPECIAL EDITION

### FROM *USA TODAY* BESTSELLING AUTHOR
## CHRISTINE RIMMER

# A BRIDE FOR JERICHO BRAVO

Marnie Jones had long ago buried her wild-child
impulses and opted to be "safe," romantically
speaking. But one look at born rebel Jericho Bravo
and she began to wonder if her thrill-seeking side
was about to be revived. Because if ever there was
a man worth taking a chance on, there he was,
right within her grasp....

*Available in March
wherever books are sold.*

# REQUEST YOUR FREE BOOKS!

## 2 FREE NOVELS PLUS 2 FREE GIFTS!

### HARLEQUIN®

### Blaze™

**Red-hot reads!**

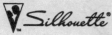

# COMING NEXT MONTH

## Available February 23, 2010

HBCNMBPA0210